Animal Heart

PAUL LUIKART

Hyperborea
PUBLISHING

ISBN: 1-988292-00-7
ISBN-13: 978-1-988292-00-7

For Emily

CONTENTS

The fiend in his own shape is less hideous than when he rages in the breast of man.

— Nathaniel Hawthorne

They all died in faith, not having received the promises, but having seen them afar off, and were persuaded by *them*, and embraced *them*, and confessed that they were strangers and pilgrims of the earth.

— Hebrews 11:13

1 TONGUE

She said kill Clay if you love me and he did love her, loved her more than he'd ever loved a thing or an animal or a person before, loved her so much that sometimes her face came to him in dreams that began before he could even fall asleep. Some nights when the hot wind blew into his open window he'd smell her. From out across the prairie, way out where the wind sheared the corn all night long, he'd smell her. Not the animals, not the shit in the fields, but her—earthy, yes, a grainy smell, but with a sweet, hollow pit that he hadn't ever smelled until he met her. He said he would do it. In the morning he'd trek out to Clay's cabin with his deer rifle and shoot him through the heart.

"Through the heart," she said. "That's nice. I like that. Through the heart."

She touched his chest when she said it, a rusty up-turned nail of a touch, one finger upon which he hung his existence.

"Bring me something. Something of his," she said.

"You mean like his hat?"

"I want his tongue."

"Okay," he said, "his tongue."

3

In the morning, prone behind an oak stump, he watched Clay step out the cabin's front door and scratch his crotch and stick a cigarette in his mouth. The little puffs of smoke drifted up and into the morning fog, the wet air that spread itself as dew on the grass that soaked his legs and the front of his t-shirt as he lay there. The crack leapt from the chamber, bounding across the fields and rolling back. Clay, struck in the guts, tumbled off the porch and inched in the grass like a caterpillar, moaning his own name.

"Oh Clay, son of a bitch, Clay."

He was upon him, flipping him on his back, straddling him where the bullet had busted into his intestines. He yanked the Buck knife from its sheath on his belt, stuck it deep into Clay's mouth and worked the blade around and around and eventually out came the tongue, a swollen thick thing with two white, stubby fibers poking out from the back. He felt stupid suddenly, standing over Clay, holding the man's own tongue. Clay wasn't dead, not yet. He blubbered and spat and flapped his arms, but the red spot on the front of his tank-top grew and soon the grass and dew were a slime of blood and he quit moving altogether.

When he gave her the tongue, at the back table at Ray's, she took it and wrapped it in a napkin and dropped it into her purse.

"Even if you were still alive," she said, "you can't lie to me without a tongue."

"I love you," he said. "I really do. I just love you."

"You fucking fuck," she said into her purse.

"I never said that to a woman before."

"Do you know," she said, "he'd tell me, all the time he'd tell me, 'I'm going to get a newspaper,' 'I'm going to get some cigarettes,' and he'd be gone for days, weeks."

"Did you hear me, baby?" he said.

"Sure, baby. I hear you. All the way I hear you."

4

2 SOMETHING TO CROW ABOUT

One sweltering afternoon, a boy, still wringing wet, walked into Byler's Bar and announced, "I sunk Danny's row-boat."

He was nobody's kid we knew, so Bill Byler, the barkeep and proprietor, made a motion with his hand, a little flick of the wrist, and simply said, "Sunk it or not, no minors allowed," but the boy didn't go. Instead, he balled up those little fists of his and said, "Danny's boat is in the Mississippi mud and I'm the one that put it there." His voice was kind of screechy and shrill and we all looked at him.

"Okay, kid," Bill said, after a minute. "Congratulations. So where's your friend Danny now?"

"He ain't my friend. I reckon, by now, he's floated halfway to New Orleans."

A triumphant look shot from the boy's wild eyes. Then he turned around and stomped out.

We all chuckled. I took a long drink off my beer. Sunlight streamed in through the dust-covered windows. I never once saw Bill clean them.

"Ornery kid," I said.

Bill was toweling off a mug. He looked up, like he was checking to see if the kid might have walked back in.

"Oh, he just had something to crow about," Bill said, when he saw it was nobody in the bar but us.

3 ANIMAL HEART

This tale starts in a familiar way. Not quite clichéd, because it really happened, but familiar. You've probably heard it, or heard something like it, before. I came home early from work one day not all that long ago and discovered my wife in bed with another man. I don't know who this man was. I'd never seen him before in my life. I have no idea how my wife met him, but I guess with social media and the smorgasbord of dating websites, it could have been in any number of a thousand ways. Besides not knowing the "other man," what I discovered was that I really didn't know who my wife was, and what's more, really didn't have a clue who I was supposed to be. Revelations of that kind come suddenly, like a hunter's bullet bisecting an animal's heart. No warnings, no preludes, no sense that anything is out of the ordinary. Suddenly, blam! it's all over. You might sprint a little ways off into the woods, metaphorically speaking, but after a few minutes, you're done for. I suppose that kind of instant end is the real tragedy.

There was no gigantic reason I came home from work early. It wasn't my wife's birthday, wasn't our anniversary, we weren't off on some big adventure or anything.

7

I'd just finished my part of a project we'd been working on, one that had kept me away from home a number of late nights in a row. Not that it matters, but just for your information my job is to oversee a small marketing team. For this project, we'd been tasked with testing John Deere advertising strategies (yes, that John Deere: green tractors, yellow deer silhouetted mid-leap). We had to find clever ways to sell riding mowers to Spanish speakers. I say "not that it matters" because I stopped enjoying the job years ago, if I ever really enjoyed it at all. I went to the office and worked hard because I got paid. The lever I pushed to receive my food pellet. At any rate, I thought both as a little reward to myself, and as a mollifier for the ever-intensifying guilt I'd felt about coming home at ungodly hours—midnight, sometimes even later—I'd leave the office at lunch time. So I did. For once in my life, tomorrow's projects could wait until tomorrow.

My wife is a stay-at-home mom, but our boys are both in school during the day, Grant in third grade and Aiden in fifth. School wouldn't be out yet. She'd be alone. I'd surprise her. We'd go for a late lunch and talk—talk about anything, talk about where we wanted to go on vacation when it finally became summer, talk about her father's melanoma treatment, talk about baseball or boats or broomsticks. Anything. I've always liked, loved actually, the sound of her voice. It doesn't matter what she's talking about. Just because of the way it sounds in her mouth, I could listen to it all day. Her voice is soft, but not the voice of a pushover. Stern but gentle. When she talked about the kids she generally leaned forward, toward me. When she talked about her family, she sat back. Always her voice swung in pleasant, musical arcs. Sometimes, when she really wanted to make a point, she'd say, "Don't you think?" Don't you think? Don't you think, David? Don't you think? I usually said yes.

Now, here is what happened: First, of course, I let myself in by the front door. You can do it fairly quietly because the door is new. I tip-toed through the living room, the den, the dining room, and, not seeing her, took off my shoes and headed upstairs. The stairs are carpeted and you can get away with cat-like steps even with your shoes on, but to be safe, I carried mine in my hand. About halfway up, I heard an odd, rhythmic, plunking sound. You will guess, no doubt, that it was the thunking of the headboard against the bedroom wall. You'd be right. The sound got louder as I walked down the hallway. Then I found the bedroom door almost shut. There was no reason it should have been anything but wide open in the middle of the day. I was confused, definitely. From the other side of the door, besides the sound of the headboard, came short moans and grunts in a kind of call and response. First, a high-pitched moan (hers, it turned out) and then a low-register grunt (his), back and forth and back and forth like this. I put my hand on the door, and then, for the briefest of moments, hesitated. Hesitated to enter my own bedroom?

My wife's white legs were stuck up in the air in a V. Straight up in the air, and she was grabbing the pillow beneath her head in both fists. She was still wearing her t-shirt, which was hiked up just under her chin, exposing her breasts. Her bra was shoved up above them in a wrinkled line of fabric intertwined with her shirt. On the floor beside the bed in an elongated pile were her jeans, inside-out, and her underwear, a shiny black pair of panties. I'd stuffed those into her stocking a couple Christmases ago with a little note that said, "Consider these the wrapping paper for MY Christmas present later tonight." I remember thinking I was being clever and sensual, manly even, when I wrote it. Draped between my wife's legs was the man I'd never seen before. He was completely naked, his skin tanned and hairless all over. Hairless except for the hair on his head, dark brown, which was pulled back into a ponytail. A ponytail! His muscular arms were locked at the elbows so they supported the weight of his whole upper body. His back was arched, his body came together with hers at the hips. He shoved himself into her, out, in, out, his buttocks and thighs contracting in the quick, efficient way a dog's hindquarters contract when it humps your leg. (That's the first thing that comes to mind to describe the way it looked. Really!) My wife's eyes were closed, and, in between those breathy moans, she was biting her lip. The man's eyes were closed, too, and from his mouth came little words that might have actually been puffs of breath that only sounded to me like words. "Uh-huhs" and "yeahs." And then, suddenly, my wife shouted, "Fuck me! Come on, fuck me, you dipshit!" The man's response was the only one any man could muster at such a command: he thrust himself into her all the harder. Needless to say, she had never, ever shouted at me to "fuck her."

Now, as I said, their eyes were closed. If they could have seen me, if you could have seen me, I'm sure I looked the perfect picture of a cheated fool. Loosened tie, glasses that had slipped halfway down my nose bridge. Hunched shoulders. Briefcase in one hand, shoes in the other. What a perfect waste. I'm glad, of course, that they didn't see me. I'm not sure what I would have done. I might have been tempted to say, "Oh, excuse me. I'll wait until you're through."

It's true that I've wasted some time attempting to shove that scene into the back of my mind. To my credit, though, relatively little time. I've had to come to grips with the fact that it will never be the past. My wife and that man together will always be the present to me, no matter how many years I live. What I've really tried to remember were the emotions I felt the moment I eased the bedroom door open and beheld what I beheld. I tried convincing myself that what I felt was betrayed, saddened, angry. All the ones you'd think a person would naturally feel upon discovering, firsthand, his wife's infidelity. Ironically, none of those feelings felt right. What I was doing was attempting to shoehorn my consciousness into some kind of emotional mold, when really, what I remember feeling at that exact moment was…nothing.

The pronounced absence of emotions in any given traumatic situation where you'd assume there to exist extremely elevated emotions is shock, I think. Now, that's perhaps a stereotypical response to the question, "How did you feel when you found out your wife was cheating on you?" "Well, I was shocked." Of course. In a way, the word doesn't have any meaning. But there is no other word to use. I remember when I was a kid in school, I must have been just about Aiden's age, my teacher, Miss Eckers, gathered us around her. She told us she was going to show us something. In front of her on the desk was a small bowl filled with water, into which she sprinkled pepper from a pepper-shaker. Then she rubbed the tip of her index finger on a bar of soap and said, "Are you watching?" She dipped her finger into the bowl, and, inexplicably, the pepper fled to the sides of the bowl. Immediately. Instantly. Every single pepper fleck. To try to describe the nothingness, the shock, the pepper and the soap are the best things I can think of. Every real emotion was gone in the time it took my optic nerves and my brain to compute what I was looking at.

As you might have guessed, something did happen next. I say "did happen next" as opposed to "I did something next," because, though it was my body physically doing something, I have no memory of deciding upon a course of action, no recollection of the motivation of my will. I think, if memories of motivation existed here, the shock decimated them. I remember vividly, though, the events. I remember those things as if I were a tourist on a cruise ship taking pictures from the deck of my eyes.

I put my briefcase down. Put my shoes down. Folded my glasses on top of my briefcase. Then I dashed into the bedroom screaming, arms flailing above my head like I was some kind of prehistoric warrior. I plunged my arms between my wife's body and the man's body, the first time they even noticed me, and heaved the man off my wife. His skin was tight and slick with sweat, the muscles in his abdomen hard. He thudded down onto the floor in the space between the bed and the wall. It was very easy for me to throw him, literally throw him, like that. All I can think of are those incidents when people report some kind of super-human strength in some kind of desperate situation. I remember reading a news article once where a boy lifted an overturned tractor off his father's chest. Anyway, as the man was hitting the floor and landing flat on his back, I was leaping over the bed and landing on top of him, driving my knee into his stomach. This propelled a woosh out of his mouth, and further stunned him, as if a crazed cuckold was not stunning enough. My wife screamed. I'm not sure if, at that point, she realized it was me.

On that side of the bed, which was my side, was an old, squatty nightstand. A bulky piece of furniture that I inherited from my grandmother after she died a decade earlier. Made of oak with a brass lining covering the thing's pointed feet, it's about the densest piece of furniture in the whole house. I grabbed the man's ears, lifted his head, and slammed it onto the corner of the nightstand. It rang with a heavy "whang!" His eyelids seemed to pin themselves back, indicating I'd terrified him. Remember now, if you can, it's as if I'm only observing this, not actually doing it. Anyway, I slammed his head down again, again, and again. His eyes rolled around but weren't closing, so I gripped his throat in both my hands and squeezed until there was a pop, followed immediately by a fleshy, scrunching sound. After that, the man was burbling. I stood straddling his body, grabbed the lamp from the top of the nightstand, and yanked it so hard the cord tore from the wall socket. I slammed the base of the lamp down onto his forehead. The lamp was made of thick ceramic and I meant to shatter it on his head, at least that's the picture that comes to mind as I recall the scene, but the ceramic was too thick. Or perhaps I wasn't strong enough. At any rate, the lamp didn't shatter, though I raised it high above my head and banged it down onto his forehead once, twice, three times, four times, five and six times, more. This produced only silly sounding bonks. But it made the man be still. I threw the lamp down a final time, the way a child throws down his baseball when his parents make him come in, the base bouncing off the man's cheek, settling on the floor and leaning, upside down, against the wall.

When that was over, I wiped my nose with the back of my hand. My chest was heaving. For what seemed like forever, I stood above the man, sucking in huge breaths and exhaling in loud, panting gasps. Blood had begun to leach out of the man's head and into the carpet, soaking his ponytail and creating an elliptical bright red halo. His eyes were half-closed, unblinking, his head turned slightly, so it looked like he was squinting to find his shoes under the bed.

"David?"

My wife's voice. The voice that I told you before I'd always loved. Now, none of the qualities I loved about it— the musicality, the softness—none of them were there. Just a raggedy imitation, like an impression done of her by somebody who smokes too much.

My wife's long legs were ivory pillars. Her t-shirt now covered her torso, the hem of it just below her crotch. I don't know if she pulled it down to cover herself or if it just unfurled when she leaped off the bed. I let my gaze travel slowly over her, from her feet to the top of her head and back down.

"Who is this?" I said, pointing at the man. She opened her mouth to reply, but before that reply came, I cut her off. "Never mind."

I walked around the bed, back to where I'd set my briefcase down. I unfolded my glasses, put them back on. I stepped into my shoes.

My wife's face was a contortion of skin, wrinkles and lines in it that I'd never seen before. She was about to cry, about to scream, about to laugh? I couldn't tell. She came toward me, then stopped and said my name again.

"Never mind," I said.

"David, ohmygod," she said.

"Would you please—" I started, but stopped myself. And I didn't say anything else.

I drove around our neighborhood, then drove around all of Evanston, then Wilmette, then Skokie. I don't know how long that took, but at some point I went to McDonald's, a place I never go, a place we're forever saying "no" to, to the boys. I ordered McNuggets and a gigantic vanilla shake. Why do I remember what I ordered? As I slurped at the shake, in came a woman I recognized, who recognized me back, a mother on my son's former soccer team. "Hi," she said. "Hi, how are you?" I said back. I made some terrible excuse for the slop on the tray in front of me, then fumbled when she said, "Well, I'm off to order some slop myself." She didn't wave when she left, white sack in hand, and when her car was gone, I got up, too. It wasn't until I was blocks away that I realized I hadn't dumped my tray. I'd just left it sitting on the table, food half-finished.

I kept looking in the rearview mirror and driving as normally as possible. When evening started to fall, when the sky became rimmed with black, I found my neighborhood again, parked several blocks away from my house, and crept along the sidewalk until I could see it. The windows were dark. My wife's car was not there. No police cars. Perhaps they'd come and gone. She must have called them and likely they were looking for me.

A brief word about decisions here. I've always been a good decision maker. I like goals. I like to see a thing I want at the proverbial end of the line, and then make my own map to it. You include certain things, you systematically exclude other things, if those other things aren't part of your best plan. You prioritize some things, and make a note to yourself to decide on other things later down the line. So, yes, I thought about my boys, to answer the question I know you're thinking. But they were safe. She could send them to her sister and brother-in-law's in Naperville while she and I sorted things out. I am very good at decision making. It's why I'd been promoted to the head of my team at work, for example. Strategic thinking skills. In another life, I'd be a baseball manager.

I took a long route, a winding loop through the neighborhood, to the Purple Line, heading back into the city. I was usually heading the opposite direction, always heading away from the city when evening fell. I can't remember the last time I rode the train into the city as night was nestling in. Throbbing white squares of light all in perfect rows and columns, situated in black buildings, which ranged in size like the line of an enormous EKG readout. It was gorgeous, and I thought how it was such a strange time to find something gorgeous. But it was. I transferred to the Red Line at the Howard stop, and rode all the way into the city's heart.

The Red Line, as you know, slides underground around DePaul and becomes a subway. As I sat there by myself, surrounded by the thunderous rattle of the train below the surface of the earth, certain thoughts began to seep in. Little thoughts on the fringes of my conscious mind, but no other thoughts were there at the time, so I noticed these little ones. Against that white backdrop of my mind, I began to imagine that I was a little carnivorous worm. But I grew and grew, and became a giant carnivorous worm the size of the train, and with a metal hide like the train, too. A very hungry worm. With vicious teeth, chomping the concrete, tearing metal, flinging aside the layers of clay below the asphalt of the city. I turned in the ground like a ravaging screw, becoming hungrier and hungrier with each bite. I breached through the streets and bored back down wherever I wanted, eating everything I saw. Down my worm's throat went cars, old folks' walkers, city busses, secondhand stores, sculptures from the park, pubs, pub patrons, libraries, skyscrapers. I rolled and rolled, gorging myself on the city, terrorizing everybody, everything, and with each pulsation of my worm's heart, I became fortified, more relentless, even to the point of invincibility. Tanks, planes, guns, bombs were all tried against me, but they were useless. I ate them, too, and I grew and grew and grew. But soon, I'd eaten everything. Nothing was left but the blazing red sun, the flattened land around me, and my enormous, bloated body. I was so full I could not move. Could not creep. Could not burrow. And there I died, baked to death in my own destruction. My mind was interrupted by a CTA announcement, and I shuddered.

"This is Grand and State. Doors open on the left at Grand and State."

So I got off.

I wandered, maybe for the first time in my adult life. I recall what I told you before about being a good decision maker, but in this moment, that part of me was failing catastrophically. So I just began walking, which I suppose is a kind of decision, though one, in this case, with no end in mind, with no culmination of accomplishment.

After a few blocks, at the place where a particular alley connected to the street, I heard music. Strange music. Or perhaps the music wasn't strange, but that it was wafting out onto the street from an alley, that was the strange thing. The strumming and plucking of a tinny guitar. Hands whapping out a beat. The strained warbling of words, lyrics that I couldn't quite understand, hovering above the cracked asphalt. At first I walked past it, but upon realizing that something was coming out of that alley other than a noxious odor, I backtracked. Hearing it again in the same place, I leaned on a crooked telephone pole and listened. Before long, I allowed myself to be drawn down the alley. Charmed down it, maybe.

The alley was filled with rusty light from a couple of

security lights overhead. Chain-link fences, chuck-holes the
size of basketballs, uniform brick walls with joints tuck-
pointed to smoothness. The music got louder, more dis-
tinct. Then, on the other side of a dumpster, in a shadowy,
recessed loading dock, were three black men wrapped in
Indian blankets and a black woman with hardly any clothes
on was pirouetting up on her toes. One of the men played
a banged-up guitar. One was drumming with bare hands
on an upturned paint bucket. The last man sat against the
alley wall, skinny legs stretched out before him, singing in a
voice that rattled with sadness.

When they saw me, they froze. My eyes met the eyes
of the guitar player. The woman stopped dancing mid-step
and kind of tipped over, then got her feet under her,
wrapped her arms around herself, and huddled by the
singer. He draped a bone-thin arm around her shoulder.
There was a bit of a smile on his face, I'm sure of it. None
of us moved. I felt wind on my face, cool wind shooting
down the alley to the street.

"You goin' to bust us, go on and bust us," the guitar
player said.

"What?"

"Bust us, if you have to. We been busted before.
Here we are."

"Wait, you think I'm a policeman?"

"Aintcha?"

"No, no, I'm not the police."

"A lot of times the police tell us they ain't the police."

That guitar player and I just looked at each other,
studied each other, really. We did that for a long time.
Then the drummer, who himself had never actually looked
at me or even acknowledged my presence other than by
stopping his play when the others had stopped, began to
hit the sides of the bucket again. His long, dark fingers
slapped the plastic in a new and gentle rhythm. Still
watching me with suspicion behind his black-eyed stare,
the guitar player began strumming. The old steel strings

squeaked. The woman crept from the singer's side like a cat, literally on her hands and knees for a few steps, then got to her feet and resumed her dance. And finally, the man against the wall, that singer, threw his head back. Out came the lyrics. I don't remember what they were, and had never heard that song before, but the words came out of his mouth as brick dust, as oil-stained gravel, as wind-whipped plastic bags that vanished over tar-sealed roofs.

"Move your hips, baby." The woman was suddenly dancing very near me. She clapped her hands above her head. Then she put her hands on my shoulders and pushed and grabbed, working me to a dance like I was a life-sized puppet. I smelled her. Thick, human odor. Of sweat, dirt. The past, probably. Things she regretted worn on her skin like perfume. When she took her hands from my shoulders, my feet continued to shuffle in the pebbles under my shoes. The song moved them. I looked at her, and in the look I gave her, I tried to pack in everything I ever regretted. Somehow I knew that's why she was dancing, that's why they were singing. I still felt empty inside, white-washed, but I wanted her to know that I remembered regretting things, too. But she only gave me a toothless smile.

"That's right, baby" she said. "That's right. You got it now. Dance."

4 THE SNIPER

The sniper, an American named Tom Conner, sat in a burned-up living room. The external wall of that little French apartment house had been sheared off by mortar rounds—German or American mortar rounds, who could really tell anymore?—when the Americans moved in some days before. Conner sat behind an upturned couch and watched the traffic circle. He'd heard from the scouts this little street corner was leaking Germans.

When they appeared, two of them, they crouched and shuffled along, and crouched and looked. They were ten yards from each other with machine guns at their hips.

Why do they wear black? Conner thought. They stick out. Everything is gray in France. Don't they see that?

He watched them scuttle and scurry.

This job is nothing more than flicking ants off a wall, he thought. And that's me: G.I. Bug Buster.

They popped up and then ducked, then leaped up, then hid. He could hear them hissing at each other.

They're talking fast, Conner thought. Kraut speak is fucked up. Geez, they're talking fast. How can they understand each other? Maybe they're nervous.

The Springfield rifle rested in his lap.

Without glancing away from the Germans, he slid it into his hands. He was slow, gentle, quiet. The rifle was cold and comfortable. In the distance, three flat booms from the mortars out in the countryside—and the Germans glanced back. When they did, Conner flattened himself onto his belly. Then he watched them from beneath the couch.

The older German closest to him was mean looking. Conner could see his sneer. The further one might have been younger. When they paused to navigate a fallen obelisk—some kind of monument—he squeezed the trigger. A little red bloom sprouted below the mean one's eye. He flipped backward and his machine gun clattered away. Conner aimed at the younger one, but the younger one was scrambling through the debris, bobbing away too quickly. He disappeared behind a low chunk of rubble.

Ten minutes passed before the young German, Peter Huber, risked a glance. And then it was a very quick one. He couldn't see from where exactly that shot had come. He could see Lehmann, now certainly dead.

I myself, Huber thought, must be lucky. Today is a lucky day to be Peter Huber.

He unstrapped his helmet and tossed it a few feet in the air. A nob of the concrete against which he was leaning, a little piece a few feet from his left ear, vaporized in a wide white puff and some shards raked his cheek.

He smiled and shouted, "Hallo, Yankee! Versuchen sie es erneut, du hund!"

There was no response. Ten minutes passed, and then fifteen, and then twenty. Huber threw his helmet into the air again. On its way back down, it seemed to spasm, then spun sideways, then rolled to rest behind a pile of bricks out of his reach.

He stared at the bricks. His heart pounded and he thought how stupid it was to have done that. He was uncovered completely now and in the crosshairs of a sniper. Without the helmet, Huber felt naked and even, somehow, embarrassed. But his heartbeat slowed, and finally returned to normal. Then he smiled again and shouted, "Was für ein lustiges kleines spiel, eh Yankee?"

Odette Blanc, ten years old, heard him from her hiding place. The church, though it had been hit, was only partially collapsed. The belltower still stood, which was a miracle, she reasoned. It was something her mother once told her: Man is spontaneous or man is logical, but God is both miraculous and reasonable at the same time. She looked down at the soldier nestled in the pieces of the town scattered all over the streets. She saw his blonde hair and thought how strange it looked compared to his black uniform and black boots.

If I could see him closer up, she thought, perhaps he wouldn't look much like a soldier. He might look like a boy in soldier's clothing.

Odette watched the boy. For a long, long time he was still. So was she. But then, suddenly, he jumped to his feet with his gun in his hands and roared and shot at the building across the street from the church. Rattle, rattle, rattle! And as quickly as he'd jumped up, he laid back down. When she looked at that building, she could see thin white tails of smoke or dust or both curling up and disappearing. The boy shouted something else. Who was there but her to hear? She couldn't understand him.

Odette closed her eyes. Her thoughts lifted off. She imagined herself on the back of a winged horse. Pegasus, her mother called it, in the stories she told.

He is strong, she thought, but very, very gentle.

She heard quite clearly the horse's snorted breathing. She held his mane. As they mounted the sky, she saw France below her fading away—smaller now and still.

5 THE EDGE OF THE KNOWN WORLD

Mice. We had 'em in spades. In our loft in Bucktown, when Susie and I first got married. City mice, not cute children's book mice. Almost rats, big as scoops of ice cream and quick as an eyeblink. Quiet, too. No squeaking. The only sound was the scratching of their teeth on our breadcrumbs and coffee beans. About 10:30 or 11:00 we'd hear them under the stove or behind the fridge and then soon enough we'd see them skittering along a baseboard or zipping over the counter. Horrible stuff. They navigated by smelling the piss trails from other mice and they dropped their tiny shit grains in every corner of the place. Plumped up with rabies, bubonic plague, hanta virus. Just horrible.

Our loft was small and the mice felt like live-in raiders. Susie's painting stuff took up the corner and most of the plate-glass window on the street side and half the wall on the other side—her easel and canvas rolls, stretcher bars, drop cloths, rags and brushes and paint buckets. The buckets were like gaping mouths all over the floor—mouths with black and red interiors, and purple and green and blue. They made me think of portals like from a sci-fi book, pits you could step into and get whisked away to different places where all was the color and shade of the dried paint lining the bucket you stepped in. But can you imagine? Dropping suddenly into a black world—no lights, no shadows. Voices maybe, but maybe they were just in your head, and no guarantees otherwise that you weren't disastrously alone for all time. I tried to use one of the buckets to trap a mouse but a) the thing was too fast and b) Susie hollered at me.

"What do you think you're doing?"

"Trying to capture the mouse."

"Not with that."

"Sure. I throw it over top of him, slide a piece of cardboard or something underneath, upend it, voila. A trapped mouse."

"Give me that bucket back."

Susie is a good painter. Back when we had the mice, she was very into abstract expressionism. I guess you'd say it heavily influenced her. That's why, she told me, she used the buckets instead of more traditional stuff like a palette or oil tubes. She wasn't Pollock-style slinging paint down yet, chopping it off sticks and paint stirrers and all that. But in nervous little slashes she was scrubbing the paint into the canvas, ruining brush after brush after brush. Shoving it into the micro-spaces between the fibers of the raw cotton duck—she'd stopped gessoing her canvases. That was cheating, she said, like selling out.

I wonder if Susie even cared that we had the mice. She never helped me fight them. The first time we saw one, we were on the sofa, she with her head on my lap, and we were watching some German movie where these angels guide people through Berlin but one of the angels falls in love with a circus performer he was supposed to be helping. Columbo was in it, too. I don't remember how it ended because about halfway through the movie, a mouse darted into the middle of the floor, sat back on his haunches just for a second, then disappeared into the shadows towards the kitchenette. We both screeched. Then Susie started laughing and I started cussing.

"Cut the damn movie off," I said.

"Why?"

"Why? Because we have mice."

"Just one."

"I'll squash it." I tramped after it, figuring it was going for the trashcan.

"Come back to the couch," she called.

"It dies," I said. "Then we're scouring every inch of this place."

The next day I went to Home Depot and loaded up on anti-mouse stuff. I got glue traps and snap traps and poison peanut baits. When I got home, I heaved the fridge away from the wall and laid down some of the snappers baited with peanut butter, plus one of the poison peanut bait stations. I slid a few glue traps under the stove and put the rest at intervals along all the walls. In the bathroom behind the toilet went the final snapper. They're such simple contraptions, a wire and a spring, a copper-colored pad with a dollop of something tasty. But pow! when those little clawed toes touch it, off with its head. When Susie got home from the art supply place, I showed her what I'd done.

"The poison is an anti-coagulant, the guy told me. They bleed to death internally."

She looked at me. "Well, that's horrific."

"And with the glue traps, they die from, of all things, hypothermia. Can you believe that? You'd have thought starvation."

"I wouldn't have thought anything like that."

"Of course the snap traps just lop their fuzzy little heads right off."

"Don't be sick, Josh," she said to me, but I said, "I'm not being sick. I'm trying to stop us from getting sick. You know they eat shit, right? Like dog shit. They walk in it. Then they come into our house."

"That's rats. This is just a mouse." Susie's voice was sad.

"Mice, Susie, plural."

Susie had a big show open a week and a half after our mouse problem really blossomed. She had it over at a little gallery near our loft. Little, but it had hosted a number of well-known artists in the past, Susie told me. Her show even got a mention in *Time Out Chicago* and was recommended in the *Reader's* Arts and Culture section. One of the critics called her stuff an abstract expressionist "mini-revival." Her parents came from down by Carbondale and lots of friends and people I didn't know, didn't even recognize. Susie wore this great black dress and black tights and she looked so slender and good. She held a wine glass and every now and then took little sips, perching her lips just so on the rim of the glass before barely tipping it, keeping her bright eyes fixed on whoever she was talking to. There was certainly no shortage of people who wanted to talk to her. She shook hands and hugged and kissed people on the cheek in a constant stream all night long.

About halfway through the show, I was standing and staring at one of her paintings, a big square of color that looked kind of like a sunset to me. She called it "The Edge of the Known World." It had yellow whorls and slams of red and orange and down in one corner the deepest blue, applied in thick blobs over and over again—I remember her explaining to me how she did it—until it captured the light and seemed to hold it prisoner. I think it was my favorite thing she'd ever painted. Suddenly somebody was standing behind me, standing close, and I turned. It was a middle-aged man, skinny and tall, bespectacled, with a wiry mustache, slicked-back hair, and a bowtie. He had on a seersucker suit and bowling shoes.

"Gorgeous," he muttered.

"Me? Or the painting?" It was a joke. He was actually standing too close.

"Hm?"

"Me or—" and then I heard myself and said instead, "My wife did this."

"Your wife?"

"Susie Brooks, the artist."

This seemed to stun him. His head jerked back and a half smile appeared and disappeared on his thin wet lips. He adjusted his glasses.

"You're married to the artist?"

"I am."

"How fortunate. Her work is absolutely stunning." He reached toward "The Edge of the Known World," or reached out for it maybe, and traced the path of her brush strokes in the air inches from the surface, flaring his long fingers in tense bursts when they came to a plop or a splatter of color. It looked like he was directing music. "Such movement," he finally said, but not to me. To the painting.

I said, "I'm pretty proud of her."

This man turned and looked at me like I'd called his mother a garbage-eating prostitute. Excuse me? his look said. Excuse me? He forced the faintest of smiles through the skin of his face and turned back to the painting.

"I'm Josh. Brooks. Josh Brooks," I said.

"Where does she work?" he said without looking at me.

"Not far from here, actually."

"I'd very much like to visit her workspace while I'm in town."

"Oh, you're not from Chicago?"

"New York. Chelsea."

"Her work space is our loft. We live there, too."

"Of course." The man's hand went to his face, fiddled with his mustache, and then he let out a breath, a kind of sigh. After a couple more seconds, he turned and walked away.

When the show was over, we hit a few bars with her friends, but I didn't see my pal from "The Edge of the Known World." Finally, we hailed a cab, but Susie wanted to walk a little, so I told the cabbie to let us out a block from home. The night was chilly and I threw my sports coat over Susie's shoulders. The clops of our heels on the sidewalk were loud and hollow and my feet were killing me inside my dress shoes. The leather had never been broken in and my feet sweated and swam around in my dark socks. Blisters for sure. I was steering Susie with an arm around her waist. She was telling me in a loud voice how happy she was that so many people had come. We turned a corner toward our building and by then she was talking about modern-day color theory—can you overlay white on white, for example, or black on black—and I said, "Sure, why not?" She gave me a look, the kind where her eyes get thin as razor blades.

I said, "That's just because I believe you can do any-thing."

"Well...I love you," she said.

"I love you, too."

And then we were standing in front of our building.

"By the way, did you talk to a guy from New York tonight?" I said.

"What was his...what was his...who?" Her hands were on her head, fingers massaging her scalp.

"This guy, this dick actually. He was tall, real thin. Shitty mustache. Looked like he swiped his kicks from the Rock 'n' Bowl."

"Oh," she laughed, "you must mean everybody. Be-sides you. And my parents."

We went in. I sat her on the edge of our bed and slipped her shoes off. Her thin feet were damp in her tights. I squeezed her toes, something that always made her sleepy. Then I laid her down and she was asleep before I could kiss her cheek, so I tucked the comforter up around her shoulders, got my Maglite from my nightstand and went to check my mousetraps. None of the snap traps had been sprung. A few of the poison peanuts were gone. But when I shined my light under the stove, there was one on a glue trap, and it was still alive. I could see it kicking, just a fluttering of the tiny muscles in its leg, one of the back ones, the only leg that wasn't on the trap. From the drawer beside the sink, I grabbed a long-handled wooden spoon and maneuvered it under the stove, struggling to keep my light on the mouse, until I managed to stick the spoon to the trap and slide it out.

The mouse was gray with a white belly and wide shining eyes, and there were several pieces of shit on the trap like black grains of rice. When it saw me it struggled so much, these minuscule convulsions, I thought it was going to rip itself out of its limbs and plop onto the floor. Just a mouse body and head then, still alive, wriggling its way back under the stove. I held it up close, shining the light right in its black eyes.

"Fuck you," I whispered and it nearly tore itself in half.

In our little utility closet in the kitchenette, next to the bin of potatoes, I kept a small toolbox. Tape measure, pliers, a hammer, and other things. I got the hammer first, but thought that'd make too big of a mess and I didn't feel like scraping mouse brains off the linoleum. Instead, I got a Philips head, holding it by the shank, intending to knock the mouse behind the ears with the hard plastic handle, a quick hit, a broken neck. But with my arm cocked back, screwdriver in hand, I couldn't do it. Not that I didn't want the mouse dead, but I didn't want to have to feel it die. To touch its death.

I could fling it out into the middle of our building's back courtyard. Nature would take its course. The thing would be dead by morning. Maybe a stray cat would find it. Or I fill up a bucket with water and drop it in. Or just put it in the trashcan and close the lid and forget about it while it starved. I wondered if this mouse had eaten any of the poison peanuts. Maybe he was already dying. If he'd gotten ahold of one, actually consumed the whole peanut, it was supposed to take about twenty-four hours. I could slide him, trap and all, right back where he came from, then get him sometime tomorrow, dead, and throw the whole mess out. But how would I know if he ate a peanut or not? If I slid him back, he might just die anyway.

Meanwhile, the thing had started shivering. This was the hypothermia? Since the mouse's eyes were black, I couldn't tell what it was looking at. I could peel it off, I guess. Put on some gloves. How sticky are these traps? Vegetable oil might help.

But right then there was a scurrying by my feet, the scrabble of tiny claws—scritch scritch scratch. I flicked the flashlight beam down. Four of them, then five, maybe six with whips for tails as long as their bodies. Standing up on their hind feet a couple of them, reaching out with their front claws and swatting at the beam. Watchers. I flinched, I'll admit it, heart leaping up to my Adam's apple. They were seeping into my house, one after another after another, like a micro army. I tripped back, losing the flashlight and the glue trap with the mouse, the light banging on the floor and blinking out, leaving me in the dark with that awful brood. I hissed through my teeth and stamped my feet to scare them back and stepped forward in the dark, kicking toward the animals. My foot came down with a quick popping sound on a lump. I groped for the light switch, flipped it on and saw that all of the mice were gone. Disappeared. The glue trap was mouse-side down, my mouse crushed, with little scribbles of red guts on either side of the trap.

When Susie finally got up in the morning, it was all cleaned up. I'd scooped the trap and mouse into a trash bag and then put that bag into another bag and chucked it all into the can in the alley. I poured bleach directly onto the mouse's blood, then filled up the mop bucket with bleach water and did the entire kitchenette floor, spreading it to all the corners and letting it slosh under the fridge and especially under the stove. I'd let it dry and then got the Lysol and did it all again, covering up the bleach smell with

Mountain Breeze. When that dried, I threw out the mop and bucket. Finally, I got the 409 bottle and sprayed it on all the counters until it puddled, wiping it up and then 409-ing it all again, this time letting it sit and air dry. We kept a tub of disinfectant wipes under the sink, and I used them all up wiping down the fridge and stovetop, and even all the knives in the knife block, the toaster, the coffee maker, and especially the microwave. For that, I got the 409 back out and went over every inch of it, inside and out, on top and underneath, until it was brand-new clean. When I finished the sun was up.

Right there in the kitchenette, I stripped down and threw away everything I was wearing. I realized I'd never changed out of my clothes from Susie's show—I'd cleaned in my dress clothes. It all went out—tie, button-down, slacks, socks, and dress shoes. Good riddance to those. They were mottled with pale spots from the bleach anyway. I tiptoed naked to the shower and scrubbed myself for half an hour straight. Susie came into the bathroom while I was toweling off.

"It smells like a chemical factory out there," she said.

"Sorry. I cleaned. After you went to bed, I saw a few more mice."

"It's not like I don't already have a pounding head-ache." She sat on the toilet with her head in her hands and her hair drooped off her forehead like curtains for her face.

"I'll air it out."

When she came out of the shower, I was on the sofa fooling with the cable remote. She was naked with just a towel in a turban wrapping up her hair.

"I love that you love to be naked." I smiled big.

"Last night, did you say something to me about somebody from New York? I seem to remember you saying something about somebody from New York."

Bowling shoes. "An admirer of yours. Too bad he was a dick."

31

"They're all dicks." She walked over to her painting stuff and put her hands on her hips. She shifted her weight to one leg, the way she stood when she was thinking seriously, and when she was naked standing that way, it made her ass perk up. Hello, I thought.

"Unfortunately, they're necessary dicks," she said.

"Necessary dicks?"

"Did he say, like, where he was from or anything?"

"Just New York. Wait, Chelsea, too."

She turned. "Was he a gallery owner?"

"He didn't say," I said, then, "He said he wanted to see your workspace. Like, come over. To our house."

"What?"

"I guess he wanted to come over."

"Please tell me you took his phone number."

"No," I said. "I told you he was a dick."

"Josh."

"He didn't have the time of day for me."

"Josh. He was probably a gallery owner. In New York."

I looked at her in the sunlight coming into the loft, silver beads of water on her shoulders, her perfectly round breasts, her smooth-skinned stomach—I loved to run the flat of my hand over it—hips, calves, ankles.

"Josh, why didn't you get his number? Or why didn't you bring him over to me? Introduce us?"

"I figured you met him, probably."

"Well, maybe. But you do realize I talked to a zillion people last night and I was nervous and tipsy?"

"I know."

She glared at me, crossed her arms over her wet, bare breasts, and said, "I need, *need* to talk to dicks like that. I need it, Josh. Need it."

"Why?"

"Oh, I don't know. So I can have a career? That I've wanted since kindergarten?"

"Susie—" I started.

"Do you even care what happens with my career?"

"Of course I care. What does that mean?"

"Hopefully he'll look me up. Hopefully he took a postcard and thinks about the show and sees the website and decides to email me." She turned, saying more, but I couldn't make it out, only the timbre of her voice.

"You wouldn't have wanted him to come over anyway," I shouted after her. "Mice, remember?"

She said she was going out and after she got dressed she did, but she didn't say to where. I tried to sit, just sit, and watch some TV but I couldn't. I kept thinking about the mouse army from the night before, those tiny marauders from hell, teensy demons sent by the devil to destroy my house. I jumped up and checked my traps, moved the stove and fridge and, seeing nothing for now, scooted them back, washed my hands, and sat back down. Ha! … Remember that game Mousetrap? Basically a Rube Goldberg machine for kids. I don't remember exactly how it worked. I remember one of the pieces—it had a lot of pieces…took forever to set up—was an orange or maybe a red plastic man. I think he was supposed to be a diver. And then this thing that looked like an upturned laundry basket slid down this notched pole and landed on him. Or, no, that was supposed to come down on the mouse. Duh. "Mousetrap." I can't remember what the mouse looked like, though. Green? Blue? Susie's good with kitsch. I'll have to ask her when she gets back.

6 DUCK BLIND

Last fall I built my own duck blind on Chickamauga Lake, and the Sunday before Thanksgiving, I hunkered down in it just as the light of day seeped over the ridge. It was my favorite kind of morning, gray and cold, and there was a thin fog lurking in the rise and roll of the hills. Some of the oaks and sweet gum trees were still holding onto their leaves even though they were browned over and long dead. I like to hear those dead leaves click in the wind. In the summer, the TVA opens the dam and brings the water level up for the boaters and Sea-Doo riders but after Labor Day they drop it down so far that most of it, at least where I hunt, is a sloppy mudflat. The little bit of water that still lays in the lakebed, on the shore opposite my blind, is only a couple of feet deep at the deepest, but that's where the ducks fly down and sit. I figured I'd augment our little feast on Thanksgiving—the grandkids were coming—and Nancy said she'd roast the fattest one I could get right next to the turkey.

When they flew in and got locked up above me, I started shooting and, first shot, I winged a nice big drake mallard. A clump of feathers popped from his side, little black splinters against the warming sky.

He flapped frantically before spiraling into the lakebed about seventy-five yards off to the right of my blind. It's hard to describe the feeling to a non-duck hunter, exactly how the combination of sensations—the punch of the shotgun deep in your shoulder, the boom rolling off across the flat head-long into the hills, and especially the silhouette of a falling duck—makes for one grand overall feeling you could sleep on for the rest of your days. Perfection. I used to duck hunt with dogs, but I don't do that anymore. For one, my dogs all got old and some of them are dead now, and for two, I like being in the blind alone—the same reason I don't hunt with anybody else.

Ducks spook easily. They'll heel up and fly off quick if they see just a flutter of something that doesn't look right. Of course, a good duck hunter knows this about ducks and knows how to keep himself absolutely still. A really good duck hunter will have figured out how to look over the still water wherever he's hunting and notice the movements out there that the ducks notice. In other words, he's learned how to see like a duck. Well, I'd been sitting in my blind about a half hour, with no other kills but the first one, when somebody appeared on the far shore of the lake. Just like that, no more ducks.

A man, a young man, a kid maybe. I grabbed my binoculars. He was wearing black sunglasses and sweatpants and a white t-shirt with something on the front of it, something red, red lettering maybe. He'd dropped down into the lakebed off the low retaining wall and was struggling to stay on his feet. He wasn't wearing boots and that was really odd—the mud is knee-deep in some places—but he kept staggering forward. I realized he was coming right toward me. The mud sucked at his legs and he threw his arms out to his sides for balance. Watching him through the binoculars, I saw he was holding a knife. Not like a skinning knife or a fillet knife, but a regular chef's knife. Any kitchen has one in the knife block on the counter. When he was about fifty yards off, I hollered at him but he didn't say anything back. I saw him get his footing on a sandbar. That black mud went halfway up his sweats and the thing on his t-shirt I couldn't make out at first was a bull's eye. Looked like he'd drawn it on there himself with a magic marker. I stared.

Suddenly he was overrunning my position, tearing my blind apart, grabbing at the sticks and pine boughs I'd tacked to the front and generally hacking away at it with the knife. I jumped out of the blind, stepped back a couple of arms' reaches and held my gun on him. Never, never, never did it cross my mind to plug him. I just wanted to keep that knife away. I didn't know what the hell to make of it, truthfully. I wasn't exactly scared. There was just a strange, heavy, rotten feeling snaking its way up my backbone.

"What the hell's wrong with you, son?" I hollered.

He said—said not shouted—and I'll never forget it, "Come on, you fucking redneck."

Redneck? Then he started swinging the knife at me. Did he not see my gun? How'd he miss my gun? I was holding it at my hip like an Old West bank robber.

What an impression I must have made on that little old woman who opened the door of that little old house. What in the world did she think of me—in the silence of the second or two it took me to find my voice—standing on her porch, blood up to my elbows, splattered on my neck and chin I'd come to see later, mud slung up all over the front of my coat and waders. Her place must have been a half-mile up from the shore where my blind was. I ran the whole way.

"There's been an accident," I panted. "Let me use your phone. Please."

It didn't take them long, not really, to clear me of any wrongdoing. I have a friend, Len Walker, who used to investigate crime scenes, first for the Chattanooga police and then for Hamilton County. He's retired now, been retired for a number of years, and hates to talk about his old job. But I called him up and basically begged him.

"Rick, I don't have that kind of pull with the county anymore. Or the city. I don't know anybody anymore. That's on purpose. I aim to keep things as they are."

I went on and described the kid anyway.

"Who knows?" he said. "One of those SPCA kids? They call them eco-terrorists. You said he was wearing a t-shirt with a target on it?"

"Looked like to me," I said.

"Might be a suicide case."

"Suicide?"

"Yeah, you know, maybe it was some kind of statement that meant he wanted you to aim at him."

I got quiet.

"But who knows. Maybe it was the t-shirt of some heavy metal band or something. Don't lose too much sleep over it, Rick."

"I already have."

I let the blind sit. Memorial Day, like usual, the TVA filled the lake back up. I sometimes fished that spot, too, and one morning in late June, I lugged my rod and tackle through the woods to the shore. The water was like a smooth, black stone. I thought about how, when they had opened the dam, the water crept in and washed my blind away. My sticks and pine boughs letting go of each other, drifting off, washing up in the mud, getting cracked in half by motorboat hulls and water skis. Maybe the ospreys grabbed some for their nests.

A couple of guys in a bass boat came trolling over the spot, waking the still water with a straight slice across its back. We gave each other weak little waves, just a little wag of the finger-tips. It's the kind all early morning men, the ones with buck or bass or duck fever, give to their brothers. "They biting?" we'd say. "How was your morning?" "Not bad. Got my limit." "Way to go. Have some coffee. Have a cold one."

Their boat whined away past, following the shoreline

around a point to my left, and they disappeared. The ripple that was their wake washed the toes of my boots. Little slaps, littler slaps, until the water was still again.

7 A WEEK AT THE NORTH HOTEL

The North Hotel wasn't really a hotel at all, but a flop-house. The tenants came and went. They were hiding from the Vice Lords. They were the Latin Kings. They'd been dropped off drunk by third-shift cops. They were drug dealers, drug users, compulsive hoarders, wild amnesiacs, paranoiacs, bums, psychos, sickos. Punk rockers who came into town for shows and never left. They smoked roll-it-yourself tobacco (cheap) and weed (the stanky kind) and crack (big jaggy blobs of amber—and they were the paralyzed ants within). They lived under subsidies or sold newspapers or got government checks and SNAP benefits. They watched TV all day, some of them. Others hiked to the library down North Avenue to sit alone reading newspapers in Polish, Russian, Thai, Chinese. They were old men who would die naked in their beds. They were young junkies with needle tracks on their arms like wit-ches' fingers. "Fireholes"—what they called the spots on their bodies where they jammed in the needles—as black and open and stinking as wintertime sewers. They were prostitutes and johns, widowers and divorcees. They were right-hand men and pimps and way-down-on-the-totem-pole bookies.

And, with most of them, their minds were maimed. They took their meds or they didn't and either way they'd sit on the couches in the lobby with long lines of drool from their chins to their chests. They'd come to confessing sins. Or they'd come to lashing out. Or they'd come to pissing themselves, little single-stream fountains in their hang-down pants, and walk quietly bowlegged up the steps to their rooms to disappear from the world for days and for weeks.

Ray, who sat at the front desk, handed out keys, monitored the alley cameras, and collected rent, watched them come and go. There were leavers and stayers. The stayers were the obviously disconnected, disengaged, disenfranchised. DIS-gusting. Mostly. They didn't have phones as a rule, and if they did, they were those free government phones, and they were always losing them or breaking them and always changing phone numbers. And it was like they collected them, like it was a hobby. Five, six, seven of them apiece, busted useless digi-shit, but they hung onto them. Maybe these stayers thought all the phones were all going to come alive one day, magically wake up ringing with calls from the president, God, Katy Perry? The other kind, the leavers, had phones they kept, one apiece, and people they talked to, even if their talk was, "Fuck you, Ma!" Fuck You Ma was somebody, somebody out there who'd eventually open her doors again and out the tenant would go, whispered into the night, a gray rumor no one would ever hear again.

On Monday night, Ghost Girl came back to the North Hotel with a tiny yellow bird in a silver cage. Who knew her real name? Everybody called her G.G. or Gigi. Pronounced the same, the latter much fancier.

"What do you have there?" Ray asked her.

"A parakeet. His name is Tom," Gigi said. Her voice was high, and it fractured when she came to the ends of her sentences.

Ray said, "No pets. You know this."

"He's only a little bird," she said.

"If I let you have that bird, I have to let the next guy in with a Doberman."

"Please." This one word rang in the lobby like the sound of a single plunked piano key. Gigi stood there, tiny, with the cage in her hand. The bird was nervous. Gigi's eyes, huge, met Ray's, and Ray stared back. And a little red flame bloomed in his heart. She had a soul.

But, "No goddamned way," he said.

Gigi looked at the cage. The bird looked at her. She looked at Ray again, who'd turned back to the TV, and while he watched it, she unfastened the cage door's latch. Out flew Tom. He darted and circled and she clapped her hands.

"Isn't it wonderful?" she said.

"What is?"

"Tommy, Tommy, Tommy! My lovely little pet."

"What are you talking about?" Ray said and she pointed. The bird had landed on a lampshade. His shadow was cast in black on the stucco wall behind it, a 2-D crow.

"Oh, what the fuck, why did you do that?" Ray screamed.

But Gigi laughed and clapped and climbed the steps to the fourth floor, her floor, with the empty cage. And there was Ray the rest of the night, swatting at little Tom with a broom, always missing.

All through the winter, the North Hotel was freezing. In the summer, burning up. When spring slunk into town or when fall rolled through, it was anybody's guess. The gaps beneath the window sashes in the rooms were almost an inch wide and the outside eased right in. The gaps beneath each door were bigger. Two, three inches in some rooms. The mice moved to and fro.

"Hey, your mouse came to see me last night," somebody'd say.

"What he look like?" somebody else'd answer.

"Black, real dark. Like me."

"That ain't mine. Mine's silver. When you look at him under the light, I'll be god-damned if he ain't pure silver. Besides, mine don't go no place without his whole family, no way."

People shoved moist towels under the doors and dirty laundry or slabs of cardboard in the windows. Mousetraps slapping to at night, especially when it got cold, was a little, percussive symphony. And when the roaches came for the mouse bodies, the stamping on the floorboards—smash, smash, smash!—was the symphony's second movement.

Gigi's room was austere. The only one who knew that was Adam the Polack. Adam was the maintenance man and he lived at the North Hotel, too. Tuesday night, she knocked on his door.

"What you want?" he shouted.

"I have a leaky faucet," she whispered into the doorjamb.

"Wait till tomorrow."

"It's really leaking." Her voice was loud in an instant, a static-tinged wail, like a keening for the faucet, the fixture, all the rusting, doomed pipes in the entire building. Adam answered the door in his t-shirt and suspenders, a cigarette in the corner of his mouth.

"Oh," he said, and his eyes popped wide, "it's you," and he smiled, breathed smoke out through lips cast to one side, fumbled for a shirt in the heap on the dresser, and began to button furiously. She smiled back.

"What problem you have, now? In your room?" Adam said.

"My faucet. Drip, drip, drip. It's kind of driving me crazy."

Gigi's t-shirt was hanging from her shoulders like a flag with no wind to unfurl it. Her blue jeans were straight, plain. She was small enough to wear teenage boy sizes.

"Okay. Okay. I come up now."

She let Adam in, pushed the door shut with both tiny, white hands, and Adam saw: A twin bed with no sheets. The walls of the room were white, the crown molding black. A little radio sat on the windowsill playing classical. That was all. It was the music that made him, just for mere seconds, think thoughts that normally resided in certain shadows of his memory, places he'd put them so that they wouldn't get sunburned.

"How long you live here?"

"Five years, I think," she said.

"You decorate maybe? Pictures or something?"

Maybe she didn't hear him. Or maybe she didn't care about decorations, but what woman doesn't care about decorations, even here? Who knows what she cares about, but it would be nice to know. Just me. Just nice for me to know. She pointed to the little sink, an ancient porcelain basin on skinny legs jutting from the wall. There were two faucets, one hot, one cold, and from the "cold" the water plopped down in a beat. The sound behind it was the faint but immutable tide of the music, another kind of dream. Adam, on a whim, walked to the radio and turned up the volume all the way. The violas, the violins, and the cellos rattled and pinged between the plaster walls.

"I show you how to dance," Adam said, and took her hand in his. Soft, cold, her fingers firm. He slid his other hand around her waist, hard as a flagpole, and brought her close—but not all the way. He stepped out with his right foot. What followed were more steps, more perfect steps, a waltz in perfect time to the perfect music. Adam smiled down upon the pale woman, whose eyes radiated light and glee and love and the shadowed things were indeed enormous, the snow-capped Tatras half wooded with beech and spruce. Tumbling rivers there in the springtime. Buck red deer bellowing during the rut. So beautiful.

But he dared only to look. Never to feel.

Here came Danny on Wednesday night, in the door with his bike up on its back wheel, a bike Ray had never seen before. The North Hotel said one bike per person, and you had to keep it in the storage room in the basement. Danny had probably seven or eight bikes and they were all in his room.

"Fuck you and your bikes," Ray said.

Danny cackled a little gruff laugh, put his hand to his heart and said, "This is how I get around."

"Try the damn CTA."

"I don't like the bus. I don't like trains. I don't like them. Why I ride."

"Ride some place else."

"What?" Danny was playing dumb. It's what he always played.

In came Gigi, and Danny and Ray got quiet. She passed. Without a look, without a sound. When she was on the elevator and the doors had slammed closed, Danny said, "Hi, Ghost Girl. Bye, Ghost Girl."

Ray fumbled with a ring of keys on the desk.

Danny said, "How long she been living here?"

"Why?"

"She must have been here a few years. She was here when I moved in. What's she do? Does she do anything?"

Ray glared.

"Okay," Danny said, palms up and backing away. "Okay."

"Take your bike out back and throw it in the dumpster," Ray said.

On Thursday, Ray added free coffee to the North Hotel's extremely short list of amenities. Ray brewed it at 6AM in an old coffee maker he'd found in an alley behind a diner. It was one hell of a find. The cords weren't frayed, the carafe wasn't cracked anywhere. He carried it home under his arm on the bus and took it back into Adam's workroom, way in the back of the hotel. With an old toothbrush, he scoured its metal until it shined, then polished it and polished it until it looked brand new. Of course, he disinfected the carafe with bleach. The thing took standard filters you could find at Aldi, so he bought a bunch and bought a couple of tubs of Maxwell House. They'd love him. And when they said, "Where'd the coffee come from?" he'd say, "From me," and then, way down in the dungeon of his soul, he'd let in a dusty, piercing beam of light.

Adam was the first to pour some coffee. It was about 6:15 AM. Ray watched from the front desk. Adam took a sip.

"Tastes like shit."

"It does not."

"Don't brew shit, I say something different." Adam turned back to his workroom.

"Fuck you, you Polish asshole," Ray mumbled.

Next came Danny off the elevator, one hand on the saddle of his bike.

"Get that shit out of here," Ray said. "Where the hell are you going so early anyway?"

"I got class," Danny said. "Class."

"What class are you in, growing a fucking pair of ears and following the rules class?"

Danny chuckled.

"That coffee ain't for you," Ray said.

"Says who?"

"I say."

Danny turned up a Styrofoam cup and poured, steam swirling up around his hand.

"What do you say, Ray?"

"I made the coffee. So, put it down. I don't want you to have any."

"What, you want me to pour it back?"

Just as Ray was about to say, "Hell yes," along came Gigi again, silent and barefooted, scrawls of blue veins rippling over the tendons in her feet. She noticed the coffee and smiled a small, weak smile. Danny watched her and Ray, who had been leaning against the front desk, stood up straight and watched her, too. She poured herself a cup, then heaped in sugar and cream, then gave it a swirl with the spoon. In came Adam again.

"Ray, you—" Adam started, but when he saw Gigi, her long white hair hanging down her back, he stopped. "Oh, good morning," he said, right past Danny.

"Good morning," she said right back.

"I wish you a pleasant day, my girl," Adam smiled so big it put dark crinkles in the creamy skin of his face.

"You too. My boy," she said, and when she said, 'my boy' she said it in a teasing little accent.

Adam laughed a low, throaty laugh. Then she was gone into the elevator. Adam watched the elevator doors close, and Danny and Ray watched Adam. Finally, Ray said, "What'd you want, Adam?"

"Never mind. I forget," he said.

When Adam was gone, Danny said, "Now, what the fuck was that about?"

"What?"

"You don't think they're…the two of them are…you know," Danny said, but Ray cut him off.

"Go to your class, or whatever it is."

"Yeah, class. GED class, Ray."

"Panhandling 101. No, wait, you probably teach that class."

On Friday, they killed a man. Somebody who owed somebody something. Didn't they all owe somebody something? A new tenant up on the third floor. Later, neighbors said they heard some hollering, then a quick dull crack, just one, and then hurried footsteps through the hall—not running, but like fast walking. Somebody came down and told Ray.

"Somebody got shot upstairs."

"What?" Ray said.

"Boy's face come off."

"Did you call the cops?"

"No."

"Why the fuck didn't—never mind."

The door to the room was half opened, and the lights were all on, the ceiling light and a couple of lamps, probably with bulbs in them that had too much wattage for the little fixtures. The hot glare spilled into the dim hallway and the whole thing looked like a showpiece, a diorama, something Ray'd have made in junior high. A lot of people were standing in the hallway, zombie-folk in ratty sweatpants, their mouths turned upward in confused frowns. A couple were old women, both bald, pinching their robes shut like this was the 1950s, but come to think of it, good, because who wanted to see inside those robes? Everybody was moaning. "Ray, Ray, who did it Ray. Ray, Ray, are we all going to be okay? Ray, Ray, help us Ray."

"Everybody get back to your rooms. Get the fuck away. Back up. Out. Shoo!"

It did look like the face had come off, or was at least coming off. There was a blackish red hole in the boy's chin—boy, because he was probably twenty, twenty-one—from which a little blood trickle had slipped down the neck and dove to the carpet. Where the bullet came out, right above the forehead, was a far bigger hole, about baseball sized. The bullet had torn the skin away from the skull in all directions, leaving a stiff flap of it hanging over the boy's eyes like the brim of a ball cap. On the ceiling and wall, it looked like somebody had been messing around with a malfunctioning airbrush. Red spray all over.

"Well, this shit will take weeks to clean up." Ray squinted and turned around in the light, hands on his hips.

"Ray, Ray, what happened?" Danny was in the doorway.

"Go the fuck back to your room, asshole."

Ray was trying to block the view of the room with his little body, and Danny was trying to peek over Ray's shoulder.

"What happened?" Danny said.

"I don't know yet."

"Is it bad?"

"Yeah," he said, stepping aside abruptly, "it is bad."

"Holy shit."

"Danny," Ray said, and Danny looked at him with wide eyes.

"We aren't pals, you know that, right? We're not buddies? Not friends?"

"What?"

"I just wanted to make sure you were clear on that."

He shoved Danny back and shut the door, and then waved his arms around and hollered and soon everybody else scattered back to their rooms.

On Saturday, nothing happened.

Sunday morning broke overcast and rainy. Drippy more like it. Water hung in the air outside in misted sheets. It made the sidewalks even grayer. It beaded up on the awning over the front door of the North Hotel and rolled off, splatting down onto the sidewalk in a brownish red square on the concrete underneath. Countless days like this had dripped and drooled off of the awning, so it looked like they'd rolled out a carpet of rust for all the tenants.

50

"Rain not stop until Tuesday," Adam said.

"Supposed to get worse between now and then," Ray said. His feet were up on the desk, and he was thumbing through a Penthouse that had come in the mail for somebody else.

"When they come clean up the room?" Adam said.

"Cleanup crew is supposed to be here today. Earliest they could come. I guess a lot of people got their brains splatted out this weekend."

"I want to patch plaster in there."

"You've got a haz-mat suit? No? Then hold your horses."

Adam sipped coffee and kept staring out the front door of the hotel at the parking lot across the street. Sip, stare. Sip, stare. Cars shot past in blurs and streaks, their wet tires on the black-slick asphalt making high-pitched peeling sounds.

"Maybe we have sun in the middle of the week." Adam shrugged his shoulders.

"Maybe. Wow, check this out," Ray said, but he didn't move and didn't show Adam the magazine.

"Maybe weatherman is wrong. WGN is always wrong on weather."

"Shit. If I tried to bend like that, I think my legs would just snap right off."

"The sun might come back before the middle of the week."

Sip, stare, sip, stare.

Then the front door burst open, and in came Danny, leading his rusty bike by the handlebars. Water fell from his shoulders like molted scales and his bike tires squeaked. Little silver dots of water clung to his scraggly beard.

"Welcome home, fat ass," Ray said without looking up.

"Fuck you," Danny said.

"You get water all over the floor, Danny. I mop just now. Look."

"Bad day to mop. It's raining. It's raining." Danny was pointing outside.

"He can see it's raining," Ray said. "He's Polish, not a moron."

"Ooh, let me get a look," Danny said, spying the magazine in Ray's hands.

"Nope."

"I think it's mine. Gimmee my magazine."

Ray held up the side of the magazine with the postage. The person to whom it was addressed was "Jimmy Cleveland."

"Nice try."

"You get bike upstairs! Dripping, dripping."

"I'm going. Just let me borrow it when you're done, Ray."

"Fat chance."

"Go! Up!"

And then the rusty elevator doors slid open. Gigi was inside, and stayed inside until the doors almost reclosed, but slipped out as they banged shut behind her.

She was completely naked.

Her skin was white as talc. All three men saw her, of course, but it was like she didn't see them. Her stiff little body turned towards the front door. When she finally walked, her bony arms glided—didn't swing—at her sides, her steps, barefoot, utterly silent on the tile. All that could be heard was the pouring rain outside. Adam's eyebrows, fuzzy arches, shot upward. Ray kicked his feet off the desk, sat up, and gasped. And Danny's jaw opened and shut, opened and shut, like he wanted to say something, changed his mind, wanted to speak, then didn't. She stepped outside under the awning. Rain fell all around her. Then she turned south and disappeared.

"Oh my—" Danny started, glancing at Adam, then Ray. He stifled a laugh.

"Watch her. Don't let her get away. Where's she going?" Ray said.

Adam shoved his way out the front door and stood there under the awning. Danny and Ray heard him holler her name, a mournful yowl, a twisted screech.

8 WHAT THE HELL'S IN HELENA, MONTANA?

The tractor brakes finally burned out in Helena, Montana, and the boss only wired enough for one plane ticket, so John flew back to Chicago to get another cab and left Jerry in town to babysit the load—a bunch of basketball shoes. Jerry had never been to Montana before. First thing he did was find the dirt cheapest motel there ever was, the Pic-A-Bed Inn, and hole up. On into the second day, John texted Jerry every couple of hours with updates. "Jer, back in Chicago, John." "Jer, boss is waiting on replacement rig from Atlanta, John." "Jer, ask boss to comp you the motel room when we get back, John." That kind of news. Into the third day the texts came less, and by noon of day four they were pretty much done with. Jerry called John a couple times after lunch. It kept going to voicemail. "This is John, leave a message and maybe I'll call you back. If you have a pair of tits I will most definitely call you back." Jerry tried the garage once, too, but the line was busy and he never called the garage again because the boss canned drivers who bothered him.

Jerry's motel room was first floor, parking lot level,

with a view of a soup kitchen across the street. A dilap-
idated structure, probably some kind of warehouse at one
point. The whole building was leaning to the left. Above
the front door was a big sign with a hand-painted Bible
verse on it and another big sign that said, "No loitering." It
looked like people were always loitering. Along the
chunked up sidewalk in front of the place was a line of
sleeping bags and backpacks, shopping carts and bulging,
crinkled grocery bags. When Jerry checked into the Pic-A-
Bed, he saw a guy sitting under the Bible verse, knees
tucked up to his chest with a halo of thick cigarette smoke
swirling around his head. Another guy was lying there
looking dead, but probably actually off in some drugged-
up la-la land. A couple of guys easily mistaken for piles of
laundry. Around the corner of the building behind a chain-
link fence were a dozen or so tents, making up a kind of
drifter tent city. The capital of vagrants. Some weren't
even actually tents, just blue tarps set up in lean-tos against
the crumbled tuck-pointing.

Around about suppertime that fourth day, Jerry was
hungry. He'd eaten up all his road snacks and the thought
of something else from the vending machine about made
him puke. Since it was his first time in Helena, Montana,
and since he didn't know where the hell anything was, and
since he was aiming to save his little money anyway, when
he saw that line of raggedy men order itself and everybody
in it face the same direction, he stepped outside, locked his
door, popped a cigarette in his mouth, and walked on over.
He fell in line as nonchalant as he could, keeping his hands
in his pockets, mostly keeping his eyes down, definitely
keeping his mouth shut. When the line started to move, he
moved with it. Inside, he got a plateful of goulash from a
slack-jawed woman with an apron on and had a seat in the
white dining room. White paint on the walls, whitewashed
concrete floor, white table tops, albeit a white scarred with
initials and cuss words and symbols that probably were
gang signs, all gouged in, Jerry figured, by the rusty knife

blades half of these people must keep in their shoes.

He slurped up the goulash quick and took big drinks off the red Kool-Aid some kid had set in front of him in a plastic cup, and just as he was about to stand up and go, somebody sat down across from him. A tiny man about Jerry's age, mid-forties, though it was hard to tell exactly for the scraggly red whiskers and caved-in cheeks. He wore glasses with one of the lenses popped out, so the eye behind the remaining lens looked huge and veiny. A Mariners ball cap sat on his head, the dark brim salt-stained, shredded.

"Are you going to eat the rest of that?" he said, point-ing.

There was a little pile of noodles and tomato chunks on Jerry's plate.

"What, you want it?" Jerry said.

"Hell yes, I want it. Goulash night is my second favorite night."

Jerry handed the plate to the little man, who grabbed it up in calloused hands and scraped it onto his plate, handing Jerry back the empty. He set it on the table and didn't touch it again.

Jerry said, "What's your first favorite?"

"Tacos." Rolls of orange slime had bunched up in the corners of the little guy's mouth and bits of goulash flipped out from between his frog lips when he talked.

"I guess I missed it," Jerry said.

"You sure did."

Jerry watched him. The little guy said, "I've never seen you here before."

"I've never been here before."

"Not a lot of new people come through."

"I won't be around long."

The little guy chomped and smacked his lips, sucked the sauce from his fingers and the tines of his fork. "I wasn't supposed to be around long either."

Jerry gave a tiny salute. "Have a good night," he said

and swung his legs around and stood, but the little guy didn't say anything, didn't even look up.

When Jerry got back to his motel room, he turned on every light and the TV, too. He called John, didn't get him, and so left this message: "How's it going with the truck, Johnny-boy? I'm starting to put down roots. Got me a little wife, had me a baby. Might raise up a real nice family here in Helena, Montana. Seriously, though, how's it going with the truck? Call me back. This is Jerry."

Hell, maybe John was on the road already. Jerry fell asleep still wearing his jeans and boots and he didn't turn off any of the lights. He dreamed he was a caveman in the mountains around Helena, and got food by pretending to be dead, waiting for vultures to land, then jumping up and strangling them and biting their heads off. He woke in the morning stiff as hell, the sun screaming through the curtains and his phone was blinking a message. Not John, though. It was Karen saying her lawyer was going to call so expect a call and not to call her anymore only call her lawyer and this was the last time probably he was ever going to hear her voice.

He dialed John and said, "Where the hell are you? This is day five now. Call me ASAP. This is Jerry."

Boy, talk about time to kill. Out on the road there was a lot of time to kill, too, but they told each other stories about high school baseball games, deer hunting, their women. John's woman left him a long time ago just like Jerry's was leaving him now. John had said it was inevitable for any trucker. When Karen called Jerry up a few weeks ago to let him know that they were through, it wasn't a big surprise. Really. He was sitting right next to John in the cab when he received the call. The conversation probably lasted two minutes. He barely said a word, as a matter of fact.

"She's out the door on you, huh?" John said.

"How'd you know?"

"Sound of your voice when you said goodbye."

John looked over at Jerry.

"My voice?"

"It changed. Got lower a little bit, more scratchy. It never goes back either. You hear me talking like this? Not the normal sound of my voice. When I got divorced, it changed to this. And been this way ever since."

Jerry laid the phone down on the dash.

"Least you don't have kids to fight over," John said.

Jerry stared at the road, face hardening.

"Hell, it's been years me and her been split and we ain't quit fighting over our boys yet. Don't think we ever will." John paused. "Maybe we'd rather fight one another forever. Loving forever didn't work."

Jerry didn't know what else to do, so he took a little stroll around that part of Helena, Montana, only in that part of Helena, Montana, around the motel, there was nothing to see or do. He walked in the direction of some tall buildings way off, dwarfed by the mountains, but after about a half mile or so, he was aching and out of breath. He sat on the curb and smoked a cigarette. Behind him was a rusted-out old asphalt plant. Across the street stretched a huge, clear-ed-off concrete pad, a couple of hundred yards square, a place he figured some other plant used to sit until somebody came along some time ago and bulldozed it away. Grass and weeds, some about three or four feet tall, grew up in green jags from the places the concrete had cracked.

Jerry tossed the butt down, then looked at the mountains. Maybe they were an enormous rock-whale family that lived beneath the surface of the earth, but had to come up for air, but when they came up they froze in place, backs arched, because the winters were so cold. It's easy to see where Indians got their explanations for all kind of things. There was some tribe who believed that the Earth was the back of a turtle and it crawled around the sun in a huge cosmic circle.

Back at the hotel, Jerry watched a *Honeymooners* marathon, and then headed over to the soup kitchen again. This time it was hot dogs. Still with the red Kool-Aid. The little guy from yesterday came in again and sat down across from Jerry.

"Where do hot dogs stand for you?" Jerry said.

"Dead last."

Jerry scarfed his down, loaded with mustard. He reached for his Kool-Aid, but the little guy grabbed his wrist. His grip was hard.

"What the hell?"

"You sure all you want is Kool-Aid?"

He was holding a flask, the silver screw top just peeking over the lip of the table. The one eye, the big one behind the glasses lens, seemed like it was pulsing.

"What is it?"

"Kickapoo Joy Juice." The little guy laughed his little head off, laughed so hard the Mariners cap plopped onto the floor behind him. Then just as suddenly as that cackle had busted out of his mouth, it was gone. The look on his face was absolutely grim, like death. "Yes or no?" he said.

"Okay."

Little Guy looked around the room, then poured a lot of the stuff into Jerry's cup, then some into his own. He screwed the cap back on and the flask disappeared into the folds of his filthy sweatshirt.

Jerry and Little Guy put away a whole hell of a lot of joy juice and the rest of the night was fits and spurts, like somebody sketched the night out on index cards and then thumbed through it over and over again. They practically fell out of the soup kitchen, a plate crashing, food splattering on the white floor. They stumbled through streets Jerry'd never seen and never planned to see and might never see again, past ghost men in doorways, stubs of orange under street lights in the growing night where they drew on rolled cigarettes and let out smoke so thick that it actually hid their faces and once Jerry said, "How come you can never see their faces?"

In some way, they ended up back at the tent city. Jerry didn't know what time it was. Little Guy was either passed out or dead on the ground beside him. Jerry, still drunk, wasn't tired. With his hands behind his head and his feet crossed at the ankles, he laid back on the hard ground and looked up. It was the kind of blackness that really did go on forever, but the blackness was pierced by so many vivid, white dots—more stars than he ever would have imagined could exist. When they talk about billions of stars in the galaxy, this must have been every single one of them. He didn't know any real constellations, so the stars came in constellations his brain made up. There were some that spelled out his name, as close to heaven as Jerry might ever get. There were some stars that bunched together to form waves, and some that made animals, like lions and charging stallions. A woman's face, beautiful with long hair parted down the middle and wrapping around her neck. She smiled, too. A goddess. And then, one by one— billions of stars up there and then think of one by one— one by one, they began to fall. Here and there at first, one would drop off and Jerry couldn't be sure if he'd imagined it or not. But then more and more, and they gathered momentum, and the sky was filled with streaks of white fire until there were more fire streaks than there was black- ness and the dark of the night sky was overtaken by the light, and the light blinded him and he'd always remember feeling really, really glad to have been blinded like that.

In the morning, Little Guy was gone. The sun was high and naked in the sky. A hot wind passed through the tents, rattling the nylon into flaps and zip-zops. Jerry breathed in dust, coughed, sat up. He looked at his shoes for a long time. Then he stood and stumbled back across the street to the motel. "What the fuck, John? This is Jerry," he said into John's voicemail. Then he passed out on the bed and didn't wake up until dinnertime. When he did wake up, he had another message, again not John, this time the lawyer, who said something about papers. At the soup kitchen there was Little Guy with his joy juice and they wolfed down the Salisbury steak, practically kissing the little flask on the way out.

"What is this really?" Jerry said.

"Mescal. Homemade. By a real Mexican." Little Guy's pulsing eye was wild.

Not too much later they were sitting with their backs against the soup kitchen wall watching the sun go down, a flaming chariot of the gods and all, shot down, slamming into the mountains, burning out and scattering pieces and parts made of gold all over the west. They were talking about coyotes maybe, when Little Guy interrupted and said, "What were you trucking?"

"Just a load of basketball shoes."

They were quiet and the sun finally disappeared.

"What are you going to do with them now?" Little Guy said.

"Get them to Chicago."

"How, by hand?"

"No, they're going—" Jerry started then just as quickly stopped. He was looking up at the starlight and imagined he could somehow feel it on his face, tiny stabs of endless warmth.

9 ALL SET FOR REAL LIFE

A broke hand is nothing new. At least it feels and looks broke. Wayne's familiar with broke hands because he'd busted this one, the right one, before. One night at Leo's pool hall, twenty-two years old, opening a beer bottle. He'd set that bottle cap against the metal rim of a corner pocket and whacked it hard. Actually heard the bone pop, loud as a cue ball smacking an eight ball. Not wanting to look foolish in front of his pals, though, he didn't let his face kink up with the pain. Instead, for the rest of the night, he held everything in his left hand and went around declaring, "That's all for me, boys, I'm hustled out." He did make sure to get good and drunk. In the morning, that right son of a bitch was locked up tight—knuckles, wrist, all the way up to the elbow was numb and wouldn't move. Almost like he'd been zapped by snake venom. And down by the pinky knuckle, it was the color of a blueberry. Wayne'd shoved his right hand into a big bag of frozen corn and drove left-handed to the hospital.

That was ten years ago. Now here sits Wayne in a lock-up cell. Drunk and not supposed to be. Wayne, the former pizza delivery guy, the body building almost champ, and now on the wrong side of a pink slip from the graveyard shift at the plastics plant. Nodding on the job one too many times. Wayne the alcoholic. Now, hold on, what is it with that damn old right hand? Little trickles of blood dripping off his knuckles, speckling the floor. It might have been from a haymaker to a fat man's teeth at Leo's. Anyway, the hand hangs at the end of his forearm like a robotic claw with screwed-up wiring.

"Guard! Guard, I got a wound!"

There's a long, skinny hall to the right of the cell with dead white light blaring down from glowing tubes.

"Hey, guard, I'm bleeding all over your terrazzo back here!"

Finally here come clicks of stiff-heeled shoes, which become clonks as they get closer and then the guard, a trim old man who looks like the gunney from *Full Metal Jacket*, is standing right in front of Wayne.

"What's your problem?"

"This." Wayne holds up his hand and the little blood river reverses direction, sliding back through the black arm hair, heading for his elbow.

"And?"

"I can't open my hand. Can't close it either. I think it's broke."

"And what should I do about it?"

"Don't you guys know first aid or something?"

"I know first aid."

"Well, help."

"Problem being, you're in there and I'm out here. You can't come out here because your ass is under arrest, and I sure as hell am not getting in there with you."

"What?"

"It looks like we're at an impasse."

They stare at each other, hard stares.

"Agreed?" the guard says.

Oh. Okay. Not a word to this dumbfuck now.

"Good," the guard says, and stomps back down the hall.

Wayne had been at Leo's watching the league nine-ball players earlier on. He's in there nearly twenty-four seven, ever since the end of things at the plastics plant—and yes, it's a bar, yes, alcoholics shouldn't go to bars, but Wayne typically orders Diet Pepsi. So, the booze tonight was actually just a one-time thing, not like a relapse. Wayne had been talking to Leo, just talking normal talk, when here came this husky stranger, completely interrupting. Made his order with some smart line like, "Make it snappy, barkeep." Leo can use the business, really NEEDS the business, poor guy, so he kept his mouth shut and started pouring. Wayne didn't like the stranger's tone, though. Didn't like the stranger. Made a remark of his own. Somebody took a swing. This. That. Cops. Jail. That sounds like what probably happened.

Those thoughts go barreling past. Wayne sits on the cot and stares at his boots. Real croc skin, a pair he stole from Uncle Dexter way back in high school, a time in the world's history when Uncle Dexter was passed out drunk mostly always. Dex is dead now, but the boots still fit. Wayne taps the toes, more click, click, clicking. His hand is turning purple and has swelled up like a toilet tank float ball. Plus, there is some sting seeping into it now. The blood drops look like some kid spilled his penny collection on the floor, except they'd have to be bright red pennies. Bright red plops of pennies. Oh. Blood. Blood, blood, blood. No, no. Here we go. Out go the lights now. Damn it. Out they go.

When Wayne comes to, another guard, a lady, is dabbing his forehead with a wet, white cloth. She's upside down.

"What...the fuck...happened...?"

"You passed out, partner."

She keeps dabbing. It feels cool, nice. Wayne's eyes flit around. Still in a cell. He looks at the lady guard again. She's squatting over him, thighs about busting through the polyester deep green of her uni pants.

"What happened to Officer Friendly?"

"Officer Henderson just went off shift and I just come on. I'm Officer Reardon."

"I want to make my phone call."

"You didn't make one yet?"

"Not yet."

"On your honor?"

"I wouldn't fib about my phone call, honest to God."

She nods, then says, "You got a banged up flipper there."

"I knocked somebody out I'm pretty sure."

"Oh yeah, who?"

"A fat-ass, as I recall. A wise-ass too. And probably a just plain, regular ass."

She reaches under Wayne's supine body, worms her hand between his shoulder blades, then, with her other hand, clenches Wayne's left and pulls him up.

"You feel dizzy?"

"Yep."

"Sit there a minute."

"Am I drunk?"

"You sure are. And that ain't helping you any."

"I am not supposed to drink."

"No?"

"I am an alcoholic, lady."

"You call me Officer Reardon."

The sound of her shoes as she walks away is different than Henderson's. More like clapping. She is giving him a round of applause for being honest about his booze problem. Me? For me? He tries to stand, but only gets halfway up before the whole cell melts before his eyes in bright colors like a rainbow dipped in vinegar. He sits down. Very gently. Very.

Hours pass, maybe days, maybe weeks. Time spent in more and more pain. The hand is throbbing like a broken heart on a spindly branch stuck in Wayne's shoulder. Something he could wave around in a crowd, at a ballgame or a concert, something he could stick up in the air to say, "Hello, World, remember me? Alcoholic, yes, but now a new man who rose up above his problems with a heart intact. A man all set for real life."

A shadow slides into the cell. Wayne looks up.

"Hey there, buddy."

His sponsor, Allen A. from A.A., stands on the other side of the bars, hands stuffed into the pockets of that damn tan windbreaker. The look on Allen A.'s face is like a person at the zoo seeing a big snake for the first time. What is this...thing?

"I got a problem, Allen A."

"I'll say."

"Look here." Wayne holds up his hand, thick and discolored, immobile.

"Looks bad. What'd you do?"

"I fell down."

"Fell down? You must have fallen down off a building."

"Okay, so maybe I think I punched a guy in the mouth."

"Actually, I heard. They called me down at Leo's and said you were toasted. They said the cops hauled you out. Who'd you hit?"

"A big-ass turd. Didn't catch the name. And right now, I'm only a little bit sorry."

Allen A. looks up and down the empty halls. "Well, it makes even more sense then. They got you for battery. Assault and."

"They won't give me any ice for this."

"Here."

Allen A. slides the Big Book out of his inside coat pocket, a mini-version of it, a little Big Book, and slips it between the bars of the cell.

"You got some time. Might as well read."

"Come on, man."

"No whining. One day at a time."

"Fine. No whining."

Allen A. goes.

Later, Wayne makes his phone call. Officer Reardon had returned, woken him (because he'd conked out again), hauled back the cell door, and escorted him up to the front desk, the furthest he had been from the cell in what seemed like hundreds of years. Wayne crash-lands onto the old folding chair next to the desk and Officer Reardon sets the gray push-button phone, with a stifled clank, right in front of him.

Wayne lifts the receiver with his left hand. He hefts it a few times like a dumbbell. Meanwhile, Officer Reardon snaps on purple latex exam gloves and Wayne watches her take his right hand in hers and cradle it, then begin working the fingers. He watches her face while she watches his hand. Little wisps of dirty blonde hair escape her tight braid and curl around her ears. He watches her touch his hand and likes it. It looks like she is forcing the fingers to do sit-ups, as if the fingers have their own sets of ab muscles. Hm. What would you call the muscles in fingers' bellies? There has to be a name for them. Anyway, he can't feel what she's doing. It all looks like a little circus act. The Amazing Lock-up Guard and Her Performing Troupe of Fingers.

Wayne shakes his head. "Who would you call if you were me?"

Officer Reardon stops fiddling with his hand. "My husband, Mike the Baker. Best cake-baker in three counties. My opinion, all the counties."

Wayne blinks. "You're married?"

"Fifteen years worth."

"Izzat right?"

"Don't be so surprised," she says.

"I am surprised, to be honest." Wayne pauses, then chuckles a throaty little titter.

She squeezes where the pinky meets the palm, a hard squeeze, and pow! high-voltage bolts of pain rip through the hand, pain so great Wayne almost hears it crackling. He leaps to his feet, just instinct, and the chair folds smashing flat to the floor. Five full minutes pass while Wayne jumps and screeches and dances and cusses. When he winds down, he's sucking air big time, wheezing really, loud honking breaths in and out and in and out, slowing to normal, and finally he ends up doubled over in the corner, clutching his broken hand to his heart. Officer Reardon approaches him like he might burst into flames.

Wayne straightens. "One time I let a guy kick me in the balls for ten bucks. I'm an alcoholic, remember, so it was for gin money. This was worse. By about a billion miles."

Officer Reardon picks up the chair and sets it up. She brushes the seat off, still wearing the purple gloves.

Wayne sits and says, "It really, really, really, really hurts now."

Officer Reardon fills a Styrofoam cup at the drinking fountain and hands him four aspirins. "You're not allergic, are you?"

"I don't think so. I am not drunk anymore either."

She's watching Wayne gulp the water and when he's done, she takes the cup.

"Well, I am married," she says and then, almost an afterthought, adds, "you ass."

"What—" he starts, but sees Officer Reardon stab a finger in the direction of the phone. She stands behind Wayne while he makes his call and when he hangs up, she grabs the phone and sticks it in a desk drawer. She puts her hands, purple yet, in his armpits and lifts. Wayne stands the rest of the way, totters in the boots back down the hall to the cell with Officer Reardon trailing behind him, pants swollen with her legs, zipping and zopping with each step. Wayne enters the cell and smudges the blood on the floor with the stolen boots and behind him the cell door whangs shut.

"Mike the Baker is a lucky man," Wayne says without

looking over his shoulder.

"He is," Officer Reardon says, then leans on the bars and says, "I don't want to see you in here again. Clean yourself up."

"You won't. I will," Wayne says, then, "Well, maybe we'll see each other at the store or the Laundromat or something."

"If they let you out of here."

"What about my hand?" he says, but she's halfway down the hall.

Wayne leans on the bars of the cell and gives a little push to the cell door, but Officer Reardon remembered to lock it. He sits back on the cot, counts the holes in the ceiling, and hears the faraway crack and roll of pool balls.

10 FREEDOM

When the bus dropped him off, Hayes wondered, "So, how far down does this drop go?" He stomped down the bus steps in old dress shoes, toting the square-cornered suitcase. He turned and, right before the driver closed the doors, gave a little salute, a "so long to the institutional life." The bus barreled away down Van Buren Street, two curls of red dust in its wake. When he couldn't see it anymore, he sat down on the suitcase and rolled a cigarette in his lap.

Suddenly he was aware of all the cars zooming by on Van Buren. Makes and models of all kinds he had never seen before. So rounded—where's the bumpers, where's the chrome?—and some of them so squat and compact that they looked like half-cars, four wheels hammered onto just the cabin. The traffic kicked up hot wind and every now and then he had to clamp his trilby to his head. When the cigarette was gone, he stood. To his left, downtown Phoenix, with glass glittering in the skyscrapers and the brown sidewalks cooking in the sun. To his right, Van Buren Street unrolled straight, stuck with palm trees on both sides—one on this side, one on that side, directly across from each other all the way to the horizon.

Hayes chose downtown and crossed the street. He'd ambled about a hundred yards when a cab pulled up. Stretching across the bench seat, one hand still on the wheel, the cabbie rolled down the window and peeped at him over the silver rims of aviator sunglasses.

"You like walking, amigo?" the cabbie said.

"Not particular, no."

"Get in."

"I'm broke."

"Where you going?"

"No place."

"You got a suitcase. You're going somewhere."

"Alright. Chicago."

The cabbie rubbed his chin. "I don't go that far."

"I'm broke anyways."

"You new to Phoenix or what?"

Hayes looked down. The toes of his wingtips were scuffed and cracked. The cream-colored pants were too short. Underneath the blazer, the same color as his pants, his shirt was sopping even though he'd just gotten off the bus where it was cool and where he'd been asleep.

"No. But I been gone twenty to twenty-five years. Let's put it that way."

The cabbie took off the aviator glasses. "Where?"

"Up the road a little. FCI Phoenix." Hayes pointed with a long skinny arm.

"My uncle spent some time somewhere up there. 'Loco Ojo' Morales."

Hayes shook his head.

"He paroled out a while ago."

"No parole in federal."

"I figured. Or else you'd have some place to go."

Hayes patted the passenger door and said, "Well, so long."

The cabbie quickly said, "Okay, right, so long."

Away went the cab, crunching stones by the curb. The guy got smaller in the rearview. The cabbie, Calderon, drove downtown through the streets that lay like dried-up creek beds between the buildings. Sunlight leapt into the cab and out. Nobody wanted a ride. He hung his arm out the window, played the wind through his fingers and, circling Patriot's Park where all the bums slept, thought about the guy again. He cut a quick U-turn through traffic and headed back out Van Buren. There he was in the exact same place, sitting against a huge palm tree with a cigarette pasted to his lip, legs V'd out in front of him. He looked like a beat-up doll. The guy's blazer was pulled down off his shoulders, but not completely off his back. 'Got to be a hundred and five out here,' Calderon thought. 'Why don't he just take it off?' He U-turned again.

"Hey, guy, come on, get in," he shouted, when he'd pulled even with him.

"I'm broke. I told you," the guy hollered back.

"No, no. No fare today. Come on, okay?"

The guy wobbled to his feet, dusted his knees and came over. He tossed away the cigarette.

"What good's a ride you don't have to pay for?" the guy said.

"It's good because it's free."

"Why don't you let me sit up front with you?"

Something tightened in Calderon's chest, a little spasm of reaction that coursed down his arms into his hands, his fingers. He gripped the wheel tighter. The guy was leaning into the cab now, looking around. He flicked the Madonna and Child glued to the dash, a plastic figurine that danced whenever the cab nailed a pothole. Calderon wasn't terribly religious—he'd gotten the idea from Paul Newman. Still, it was supposed to be sacred.

"So, where you going to take me?" Hayes said.

"You got a place to stay?" Calderon said.

The guy stood up. "Nope."

"Well, I'll take you to a place you can stay."

"How many times I got to tell you, cabbie, I ain't got no money."

"Calderon. I know a place. The guy'll put you up, at least for tonight."

The guy leaned in again. "What is it, like some kind of whorehouse?"

"No, it ain't a whorehouse. It's a motel."

"One of those crackhouse motels?"

"Just a motel."

Hayes stroked his cheeks. He felt his whiskers, sharp and thick. He thought about how they were gray now. When he used to shave every day they were still brown with a frost of red. Now that he only shaved when he thought about it, the color had given out. He glanced up and down Van Buren and swore that somewhere around here, maybe off one of these side streets, there was a mission, some kind of shelter. A little place an old cellmate said he was getting paroled to. Of course, that was some years ago and maybe they'd knocked the place down or maybe it wasn't even real.

"Yeah, okay," he said finally. "Call me Hayes, Señor Calderon."

The place was the Desert Inn, a one-time motel to Midwestern middleclass vacationers in the 1960s and '70s. A big, square plot of concrete upon which a low, flat-roofed, three-story building sat. It occupied three fourths of the concrete square in a rigid, backward "C" shape. Cut into the ground on the fourth side was a pool, but there was no water in it, only a pile of browned palm branches and squeezed, silver beer cans. The motel's sign, the original, was dented and cracked, but still named the mid-20th-century amenities: "Color TV! Air Conditioning! Complimentary Coffee!"

"Wait here a minute." Calderon got out.

"You worried there ain't no vacancy? Too many movie stars?"

"Beats the motel you been staying at, don't it?"

"True. I suppose."

"You suppose. Hold on."

"Tell 'em I want the mouse-est free-est room," Hayes hollered, but Calderon was already gone in the office.

Hayes looked around. The low, stucco walls around the pool, dividing the property from the sidewalk, were pink. The whole motel was painted pink, or maybe had been stained pink after so many years in the desert sun and wind. Crinkled up Funyuns and Flamin' Hots bags were piled in a little drift of litter against the wall closest to the cab. Up on the balcony above the office, a huge man sat in a tiny plastic chair, watching the parking lot. He sat in the shade of the awning with his hands folded on top of his gut. 'Whaddya say, Fatman?' Hayes thought. 'Looking for your girl to come strolling on up?'

Out came Calderon, a bounce in his heels. Behind him was a short, squat man with a thick mustache dyed black. It hung down the sides of his mouth and hid his lips.

"Okay, let's go," Calderon called, and Hayes got out with his suitcase.

"This is my friend Fred Marchand, Freddy Marco. He manages the place. You got a room for a week. You're in," and here Calderon looked down at the key in his hand, "two thirty-three." He handed the key to Hayes.

"Coffee in the lobby here twenty-four seven," Freddy Marco said, and his dark eyes ran up and down and up and down Hayes' droopy body.

Hayes turned back to Calderon. "Well, thanks for, you know, thanks for the lift. And thanks for this." He made a sweep with his bony hand in the air above his head. They shook hands. Hayes took three or four steps backward toward the concrete stairs, then turned and climbed them. He was bowlegged and each time his heels hit a step, clonk, clonk, clonk, tremors coursed up the stalks of his legs.

"He doesn't look like much trouble," Freddy Marco said.

"I'll be by on Wednesday with the balance," Caldron said.

"You know where I'll be."

Calderon backed his cab out of the parking lot, creaked back to Van Buren Street, and rumbled away.

Having a key was new to Hayes. He looked at it, an old gold key with brown stains down inside its ridges. A red, plastic, diamond-shaped key fob, like a big tail, clacked against the doorknob. He had to force the key and shoulder the door open and the stale air inside absorbed him. Sunlight sliced through the vertical blinds where motes were rising, each particle a tiny, glowing, bird-shaped thing. They rose toward something heavenly, called skyward by the tug of the dust god. But the door whumped closed and then the dust was a billion flakes of human skin, the majestic sky a ceiling with orange water stains. Hayes stuck his hand out the door, yanked his suitcase inside and threw the deadbolt. Still in his clothes and shoes, he collapsed onto the bed and fell asleep.

He woke up sure he was dead. It didn't matter if he closed or opened his eyes, because all was black. 'I'm in hell,' he thought, 'what I was afraid it was—nothing and nobody.' He blinked and blinked harder but the black emptiness before him became more black emptiness and he sat up gasping like he'd been stuck under water. The sound of his heart in his ears, like somebody hammering on a sheet of steel, was how he finally knew he was still alive. He listened to it for a long time, listened to it slow and fade. And his eyes adjusted. All the black became a charcoal haze and a streetlight glowed through the blinds. Night, but he didn't know what time it was. It was the same way he woke up every night in prison for the first year he was locked up.

In 1988, all the money in the United States was locked up like seawater in the ice caps, in the banks, company vaults, even in the checking accounts and portfolios of slick-faced men who manned those banks or ran those companies. Toward the end of the decade, even though it was all supposed to be trickling down to the joes, the trickle was caulked and sealed. Hayes and June, his wife, had come to Phoenix for work, came from Chicago like the snowbirds out in Surprise and Youngtown, bought a little house on 13th and Fillmore, a fixer upper in gangland—what they could afford with all their savings—and they loved it at first. Hayes went out to look for work, anything available—warehouse, mechanic, plumbing, electric. He could drive a forklift, weld and solder, lift, load, unload, lay asphalt, run a jackhammer, chop, mow, in the sun, in the cold, alone or on a crew, for union wages or cash under the table. He came, cap happily in hand, smiling bright as a desert sunrise.

At night, he worked on the house. The huge swamp cooler that sat on the roof and should have been pumping cool, moist air through the ducts hadn't worked for months. The guy who owned the house before them had told them so. At least he was honest. Hayes oiled the motor, replaced the pump tubes, scoured the rust away, put in new filters. After a few days, it was working. But then there was an early-summer desert squall, where bursts of wind and rain bowled over rows of palm trees and the barrio streets became grimy rivers. The thing quit again, this time for good. They'd pledged then, Hayes and June, to weather the summer heat with only their box fans, but after three nights of zero sleep they bought a new cooler, a smaller one, from a junk man. It set them way back. And work had become harder to find, his kind of work. When worse had come to worst, at least worst so far, Hayes was waking at 3AM to get a day-labor ticket. When he finally made it home, it was usually dark and he could barely stand. Mid-summer the new cooler quit.

The idea to break the law tumbled in through this unrelenting landscape. He'd wondered about June. 'Should I tell her, shouldn't I tell her?' and, in the end, he didn't. He bought a .38 off a junkie in an alley near the day-labor office. It cost three weeks' wages. Hayes had grabbed the junkie's bony arm and escorted him to the other side of a dumpster.

"What the fuck, what the fuck, please don't hurt me, please don't hurt me," the junkie mumbled.

"I ain't gonna hurt you," Hayes mumbled back. "I seen you hanging around here all the time. I know what you do, what you want. Maybe we can help each other."

"What the fuck, what the fuck?"

"You can get me a pistol. Una pistola?"

"What?" The junkie's eyes were red-rimmed and wide enough to pop out of his skull. Hayes jerked the arm.

"Listen. Who can I get a gun from? You? Find me a gun. How much?"

The junkie's eyes narrowed. "Three hundred."

"Make it fifty."

"Three hundred or I tell the undercovers you tried to buy a gun off me."

Hayes jerked the arm again and the junkie was as limp and loose as a Raggedy Andy. But there was nothing else Hayes could do.

"Tomorrow, this time. Right here. Bring bullets, too," Hayes said.

"You got a permit? I do background checks." The junkie laughed, a high, coughing whine. When they made the handoff the next day—two paper sacks—the junkie said, "So, how come you didn't just go to a pawn shop?"

Hayes blinked.

"Easier there. Less danger." The junkie turned back toward the alley, but said over his shoulder, "Let that be a lesson to you, young Grasshopper."

Things went quickly at the bank. Hayes pulled a stocking over his chin and in he charged, firing two into the ceiling before making his demands: "All of it. Even the pennies. Hurry up!" While the white-faced teller was filling a deposit bag and everybody else was facedown on the floor muffling their screams, a security guard was creeping up on him from behind. The teller topped off the bag and whispered, "That's all there is."

The guard leaped. The gun went off. The teller's head exploded. Minutes later a thousand cops were trampling all over him, bending his arms and legs like he was made of bread dough. He remembered the pink and black terrazzo tile, how all their shoes click-clicked as they forced him to a squad car. After ten years locked up, June's visits suddenly stopped, and in the eleventh year, he got a letter. She'd gone back to Chicago.

Fourteen years ago and counting. Hayes rubbed his eyes. He couldn't bring June's face to mind anymore—she was the concept of a spouse now, an ideal to which he still considered himself dedicated. He was just about to imagine her voice when instead he heard the doorknob to his room rattle. He stared at it, stared at it, a light spot with a rim of a shadow in the dark. Then the door popped open. Just an inch. After a few seconds, it slowly opened wider, a black fissure. Somebody had cut the lights in the hall. Hayes was on his feet, tiptoeing toward whoever it was on the other side, when he saw an arm shoot out from the crack, striking like a rattlesnake the handle of his suitcase, grabbing it and snatching it away.

Hayes was instantly out the door, turning after the wild footsteps. Ahead of them, the dim arc of a flashlight beam caromed off the walls and ceiling. On a dead sprint, Hayes crashed into the thief and they tumbled to the floor, the flashlight and suitcase clattering away. The culprit groaned and Hayes heard panicked shuffling as whoever it was kicked out in all directions. Hayes grabbed the flashlight. Brown slacks, a white button-down shirt. The face. It turned into the light. A thick, black mustache. The cabbie's pal, Freddy Marco. Hayes threw the flashlight at him, bonking him in the forehead. Freddy Marco hollered, the light went out, and then Hayes was on top of him, a flailing fist to jaw, fist to neck, to jaw, cheekbone, jaw, jaw, nose, nose, nose until the nose crumpled completely, jaw, and then Hayes was on his feet. He couldn't see anything again, and this time the only sound was his own ragged breath.

Hayes gave Freddy Marco a little kick, and it was the feeling of kicking a sack of sand, soft and soundless. Hayes felt along the wall of the hall until he came to his open door. He toggled the light switch off and on, loud whacking clacks in the dark, but it didn't bring forth any light. 'He cut the whole damn wing,' Hayes thought. He yanked back the blinds, unlatched and threw open the window and screen, and climbed out.

The "occupied" light was on, but there were no passengers. Calderon liked the vague blue feeling late night driving without passengers gave him. Besides, nobody was hailing a cab at 1:30 AM. Those who were home were home, tucked in, locked up tight. Those who were out weren't done being out, not for another couple of hours. He'd collect them then. Mostly drunks—rich and loud and chubby. He'd drive them home or to hotels or to pay-per-hour parking lots, where they'd then drive (dangerously) home to vacuous mansions in Scottsdale. Or fornicate in fumbled strokes on their passenger seats, fat men with their underwear only half down when they finished. And their tiny women would re-clasp their bras and wipe their hands on leather armrests.

He drove way out to South Mountain. The wind coming in the open window had cooled. The dusty, weedy smell of creosote swirled the human smells from the backseat upholstery—vomit, residual cigarette smoke, worn-out cologne whose throat-stinging reek was a picked-clean skeleton of Eau de Desperation. He circled in one of the visitor parking lots and drove back the way he'd come. Calderon owned the cab outright now and set his own hours. And since there was nothing else to do, Calderon set a lot of hours for himself.

"When you reflect on your life so far, what do you see?" his sponsor had once asked him back in the early days. Calderon had no idea then what that meant.

"Reflect like, what, like a mirror?" he'd asked.

When he looked back now, Calderon saw these things: A much younger version of himself with thick black hair soaked and combed straight back, a little turned-up tail at the nape of his neck. A white tank top. Muscles in his chest and arms. Jessica, his new wife, standing behind him, pink nails leading her fingers over his shoulders, his elbows, then to the small of his back and around to his stomach. That landed them quickly in bed, but when she reached for him, he said, "Watch my hair, baby. I just got it right. Don't touch."

A few years later, he saw himself in a pay-by-the-hour flophouse. Light, barely any, was coming from a little blue tabletop lamp. The whore poured whiskey on her bouncing breasts and he lapped it off. After he'd finished and after she'd fallen asleep, he'd fumbled in the dark for the bottle and drank the rest in a few quick gulps.

He loved booze. He loved women. But Jessica left him when he was stone-cold sober. He'd quit drinking for two or three weeks, and had gotten some work loading delivery trucks at a food bank. This was the 80th, 90th time he'd quit for good. He'd come home to their little downtown house, a dirty one-story stucco structure with a caged front door, the whole thing the color of desert sand, like a hollowed dune the wind had whipped up and dropped into the roughest neighborhood in Arizona. He was cheery that day, had greeted her with something like, "Hi, hon, how are you?" and meant it and kissed her brown cheek, but she hadn't kissed him back.

"Why no kiss?" he said.

"I don't kiss men I don't love no more." Her voice was even, solid. Not a hint of panic. Completely confident. Calderon remembered her confidence and how it had shaken him. Above all else, above his tenuous sobriety, above the bone-crunching feeling of rejection, above the eventual loneliness and the pits of depravity, it was her confidence that day, her utter certainty, that most disturbed him. Because, he knew now, but didn't know then, he himself had never been confident in his life.

"Come on, baby." He approached her, arms out, a half-smile.

She didn't respond, though her black eyes penetrated his.

"Okay," he said. "Why don't you love me anymore?"

"I mailed you a letter. It's all in there. Read it."

"Where'd you mail this letter?"

"To here."

"You mailed a letter to me at my own house?"

"That's right, your own house. You. By yourself. In this house." She turned quickly, a little pivot with her whole body, and her purse was on her shoulder. She was holding her key out to him.

"What the fuck, baby, come on."

She tossed the key onto the couch.

"I'm doing good, baby, doing real good. Working, quit drinking. You wanna go on vacation? Let's go to San Diego."

She was striding to the door, which he'd left open.

"Hit me," he said. "Come on, I want you to slap me as hard as you can. Right across the cheek. I won't stop you. Hey, you can even have my good side, huh? Real hard, as hard as you ever hit anything in your life, go ahead. Use your nails, leave a scar, I don't give a shit, just fucking hit me."

"Goodbye." It sounded like she was saying goodbye to a salesman who'd interrupted her dinner with a phone-call pitch for a new set of knives, a vacuum cleaner, home-owner's insurance.

What he saw next became smudged and cracked. "Next" was a blur, a black whirlwind. Next was plastic vodka tubs and homeless shelters, hospitals, flophouses,

panhandling in ripped jeans by the ballpark, begging to
suck a dick for booze money, urine on his pants, the same
ones, every morning, morning after morning in the blazing
sun. Finally a suicide attempt, but the gun went off as he
was bringing it to his head, firing the bullet through the fat
of his thigh. There was a psych ward, there was medi-
cation, a halfway house, there was a sponsor, there was
sobriety, the kind that had lasted so far on into the years,
though it always felt like standing on a tiny, narrow ledge.
Which is why Calderon thought, why he reflected now.
And whenever he did this sort of reflection, usually while
driving, a sweet pit glowed in his chest—a ball of warm
relief and fear, the reverent kind, and gratitude and all of
it—taken as a whole—he assumed was God. Or maybe a
version of Him.

Calderon found himself on a stretch of Van Buren
Street again, Van Buren on the west side of the city, the
"streets" side of town. In his headlights now were the
night people. The woman in her forties, maybe fifties, in
the bright red dress, waiting by the bus stop for a john.
Slope-backed men standing in little clumps, the cherries of
cigarettes glowing, their only light. They darted away from
any other light source, like his headlights, a huddled little
mass taking cover in the shadows. 'Like deep-sea fish,'
Calderon thought, 'old, wrinkly fish.'

And then a fish he recognized, darting in and out of
his headlights, white-blue and lost to black just as quickly:
a skinny, bent, toothless barracuda. Truth be told, Calderon recognized a lot of them out this way, even knew some
of their names, and one or two he might call friends. Some
had sat in his cab before, some he'd driven around all night
so they could sleep or sleep it off, whatever "it" happened
to be on whichever given night (and often "it" was more
like "them"). Some he'd seen once, some many times,
some he'd dropped at busted houses where their families
lived (and some of those were back in his old neighborhood), and some, on his own dime, he'd checked into the

Desert Inn.

Calderon slammed on the brakes, wheeled into the parking lot of a little strip-mall, headlights highlighting words like Pawn, Lavanderia, Mart, and around he went again, after Hayes. Hayes was shambling along the sidewalk in the dark—no squared-off suitcase this time, no longer wearing his jacket. The cuffs of his sleeves were turned up. Calderon pulled into a parking spot on the street ten or twenty yards ahead of Hayes, got out, and half-jogged over to him.

"What you doing out here, vato? Why aren't you at the hotel? Come on, let's go," he said, and turned back to the cab, leading him, he hoped, to the cab, too.

But Hayes stopped. He looked down at his shoes, could barely make them out in the night. The walk just now, a few miles maybe, fueled by booze, had further shredded them and he was sure that by morning he would walk straight out of a sole. Calderon trotted back to him, grabbed Hayes by the shoulders.

"Let's go," Calderon said. "It's dangerous out here."

"My old pal the cabbie. You know, about a mile back, I swore I was going to kill you, cabbie. If I ever saw you again, I swore to myself I'd cut your head off," Hayes said. He looked up. "What's your name again?"

"Calderon. What are you talking about? Why aren't you at the hotel?" Calderon let his hands drop.

"Your buddy back there at the chateau, he ripped me off. It was a real pro job. He waited till it got dark, you see, cut the lights out, came into the room when he figured I was sleeping. But I wasn't sleeping, Calderon. Listen. Something woke me up. Hand of God, maybe? Hand of Mary, at least."

"Yeah, but why would you want to kill me?"

"You're in cahoots with him. I figure you round up guys like me and drop them off at the Ritz-Carlton back there. He fleeces them and then you split the take. What, fifty-fifty? Maybe you got the harder job. I guess you got people skills. Sixty-forty? Seventy-thirty? You drive a hard bargain, Calderon."

"No way." Calderon studied him. Hayes' head hung down, his neck limp, like a broken hydraulic lift. "Are you drunk?" Calderon asked.

"No," Hayes said. "What business is it of yours anyway?"

"You are drunk."

"I'm not going to kill you, Calderon. I changed my mind. You can live, you can live. But I'm a killer, Calderon, don't forget that. Don't forget that once in your life, out among these streets—" Hayes' voice rose quickly, and then he was shouting and turning, arms raised. "Among these streets, I pardoned you!"

Then his knees buckled and he collapsed to the sidewalk, landing in a sitting position like a skinny, starving, worked-over Buddha. A look of complete amazement was on his face. A couple of the groups of skinny fish were lurking closer.

"Come on, stand up." Calderon grabbed Hayes under the arms and hoisted, dragged him to the cab, shoved him into the back seat, and off they drove.

"Don't take me back to that hotel," Hayes mumbled.

"Why not? I gotta take you back, where you going to go?"

"Don't take me back," Hayes shouted. "Don't take me back there. I don't want to go back. I'll kill you. I don't ever want to go back."

"Okay, okay," Calderon said. "Okay."

Hayes tumbled to his left and passed out then. Calderon drove and drove, out of the city, out past Tempe and Scottsdale. Every now and then, he turned back to check on Hayes, who slept on. Eventually the rim of the world at the edge of the desert glowed, then ignited, then became a flood of fire which rolled toward them at unimaginable speed.

11 THE PLEASE HELP GUY

I'm talking to Wade. We're at Murphy's, having a few beers. The ballgame is going on across the street at Wrigley and Murphy's is pretty full. They have the game up on those flat-screen TVs. Wade's a real man's man. Baseball and beer suit him well. The Cubs are tanking in the 6th and we're mostly just talking.

"Mike, you know that guy in the wheelchair over on Addison with the 'Please Help' sign? The guy with the messed-up face? You know how much he makes every home game, just sitting there?" Wade says.

"What are you talking about?" I say.

"You know him?"

"Yeah, I know the guy you mean."

"Around three hundred dollars a game."

"How do you know?"

"I asked him once."

"You asked a homeless guy in a wheelchair how much he makes begging for change?"

"It's a racket, man."

"It might go deeper than that."

"Yeah, sure it does."

"He's got his problems. He probably had a stroke or

something."

Wade takes a long drink and says, "Maybe I'll get me a wheelchair and a little 'Please Help' sign."

"And have a stroke, too?" I say.

Wade doesn't hear my little joke. He's looking at the TV. Wade used to be married to this girl called Mary, but she kicked him out a couple of years ago. Kicked him out for drinking too much I think, but Wade didn't stop drinking. He actually started to drink more. I don't think he's talked to her or seen his kid by her for a couple of years. He never talks about that. He talks about every other goddamn thing, but never about Mary and their kid. I kind of wonder if he goes home at night and has a little picture of them on his nightstand that he cries over. I can picture big fat tears rolling down his leathery face. I feel bad for thinking that and so I look up at the TV too. The Cubs are plain doing nothing.

Right then Padre comes in. He gets two beers and sits at the table with us. He lifts one of the glasses and says, "Wade. Michael," and then drinks about half of it. Padre always calls me by my entire first name. When he starts to get really drunk, sometimes he calls me Saint Michael the Archangel. I kind of like the sound of it. Padre's a real sad story. He's an ex-priest who got canned by the Vatican for drinking the communion wine. Inside the church and outside the church. As I understand it, they—the Catholics—didn't used to care so much about that back in the old days. My father, may he rest in peace, went to Catholic school up on the Northwest Side. He said all the priests were alcoholics. That's why he never stuck me in Catholic school, I guess. Now that they're cracking down on priests because of the pedophile mess, I guess they were afraid Padre was going to get wasted and get in bed with an acolyte. Padre's not like that with kids, though. He's just a drunk.

We're all a bunch of drunks, if you really want to know. I'm starting to get worried about it. Maybe we are becoming real alcoholics. None of us have anybody to come home to. Like I said, Wade doesn't talk to his family at all. Except for a hippie cousin in Colorado, mine are all dead. Padre, the problem is, when you're a defrocked priest, nobody ever wants to talk to you again, Catholic or not. So we sit at Murphy's pretty much every day and drink beer together. It's where we met. You might call it a little fellowship, and there might be something romantic about the sound of that—I thought so myself at first—but I'm definitely having my doubts. There's a break in the ball-game and a commercial comes on.

"Hey, Padre, you know that guy in the wheelchair by the stadium on Addison?" Wade is still on this guy.

Padre looks up. He kills me sometimes. Like, he breaks my heart. I look at him and then I look away. He still wears black button-up shirts all the time and sits up straight. He's probably in his mid-forties. Not that old. He says all he ever wanted was to be a priest. He still plays one in the bar.

"Which guy?" Padre says. He crosses his legs.

"The paralyzed guy who collects change from all the fans?"

"Who is this, now?" Padre says.

"Wade's talking about the homeless guy with the sign who sits down on Addison by the stadium. With the 'Please Help' sign. He's there every home game. You know which guy he means?"

"Okay, yes. I've seen him. What about him?"

"You know how much he makes during a single ball-game?" Wade says.

"Panhandling?" Padre says.

"Mike doesn't believe me. How much do you think he makes?"

"I don't know. Thirty or forty dollars or so."

"Three hundred dollars. A game. What a steal. Just for acting like a bird with a goddamn broken wing."

"Language, Wade," I say.

"What does Padre care? He's not with them anymore. Fuck, fuck, fuck, fuck, fuck, right Padre?"

Padre looks up at the TV. He takes a long drink off his beer. I know he's just hanging around me and Wade because nobody else will hang around with him. Hell, I hang around Wade and Padre because I'm too shy to talk to anybody else. I'm not shy after I get a few in me, mind you, but up until that point, my trap is generally shut. I don't come to bars to meet women, you see. Can't do it. I come to Murphy's because it has beer. I take a gulp of mine. It's cold and it tastes good.

"What is your point with this man?" Padre says.

"My point is, the guy isn't really poor. Three hundred dollars a game. Only the players out on the field make more. But he sits there every day, fuckin' pretending. And people buy that bullshit and throw him a little coin, and eventually, he's rich. But he's got to keep up appearances, you know, so he can't buy nice clothes and he can't buy anything else. He's got to keep looking poor, or business will go bad. It's a bad racket."

"Why does it upset you?" Padre asks.

"Yeah, why?" I say.

"Doesn't it piss you guys off? He's taking advantage of everybody."

"Not you, clearly." Padre has a subtle way of standing up to Wade, but Wade usually misses it.

"That he would try to do it in the first place. That's what pisses me off."

"What if he's just trying to make a living like everybody else?"

"Well, do it honest, that's what I'm saying. Don't rip people off. Don't fake like you're a goddamn quadripleg-ic."

"He can move one of his arms and one of his legs," I say.

"What's your point?"

"He's not quadriplegic."

"What's quadriplegic, then?" Wade says.

"That's when you can't move either of your arms and either of your legs," Padre says. "Total paralysis."

"Oh."

"You learn something today, Wade?" I say.

"I thought it just meant paralyzed," Wade says.

"There was a parishioner at St. Thecla's who was quadriplegic. I used to have to serve her the Eucharist. I had to tip the cup way back for her, and she always only got a drop of the wine. And I had to break the host up into really small pieces. But she was always there," Padre says.

We get quiet for a little while. I look at the TV again. It's the seventh inning stretch. A high-school baseball team from the suburbs is leading "Take Me Out to the Ballgame." Inside the bar, we can hear everybody in Wrigley singing along. Wade sings along, too. He says, "Buy me some peanuts and cracker jacks. AND BEER!" His voice is really loud. Murphy's is full, though it isn't as crowded as it is for some games because the Cubs are losing. People are looking at us.

"Shut up," I say.

Wade laughs his head off. Padre is trying not to pay attention to Wade, I can tell.

But, for some reason, now I can't stop thinking about the guy in the wheelchair. I wonder what he does when he's not at the ballpark panhandling. I wonder if he's really homeless. Does he stay somewhere? I wonder if it really is all an act. I hope it's not. I don't hope the guy is poor and homeless, I mean I hope he's not putting it all on, like Wade says he is. I picture the guy rolling his chair up under the el tracks at night. He's got a little bag of food with him that he bought with the money he made panhandling. He shoos some pigeons out of his spot. They don't move very quickly, these pigeons, so the guy tosses some bread from the bag, only he can't toss it that far because of the paralysis, so the pigeons flock around his chair. He's trying to eat and it's getting a lot darker out. He plans on eating and going to sleep, but the problem is, once he's done eating and he wants to sleep, the pigeons are still swarming him and anyway he has a hard time falling asleep sitting straight up in a wheelchair. He finally says screw it to eating, and he leans way over to one side, as much as his crushed body can lean, and then closes his eyes. Pretty soon a long line of drool is coming out of his mouth. Pigeons have perched on his lap and his shoulders. They're pecking at him for more food, but the guy is used to their pecking by now because this is what happens every night. One pigeon, though, one ballsy pigeon, creeps up his shoulder right by the guy's neck, and pecks him right in the eye. The guy wakes up screaming and flailing his good arm at the birds, which causes the whole wheelchair to tip over and dump the guy out on the dirt. There's nothing he can do about it, because he can't set his chair back up. Nobody else is around but the pigeons, but they see this guy can't feed them anymore, so they strut off. And then the guy realizes that down on the ground, he has to worry about rats.

"Hey, you shouldn't talk about that guy the way you do," I say.

Mike and Padre are looking at the game now. The Cubs, it seems, have started some kind of rally. They've got a couple of guys on board. There is only one out.

"Are you still talking about him?" Wade says.

"You're the one who keeps talking about him. I'm just saying you shouldn't talk about him the way you do."

"Who gives a shit?"

"I give a shit," I say. "Padre gives a shit."

"Is that true? Padre, do you give a shit?"

The first two beer glasses sit empty in front of Padre. He's gone to the bar and gotten two more. He's halfway through the first. Padre looks at Wade with this really intense glare.

"I guess you give a shit," Wade says, "or else, you just don't want to say, 'I give a shit.' You don't have to say 'shit,' Padre. You can say something else. Crap. Poop. Do you give a poop about the guy, Padre?"

Wade is always making fun of Padre.

"He's a homeless man. A man who is without a home. Try to imagine that, Wade," Padre says.

"He's a homeless con man."

"So what?" I say.

"So what's the point?" Wade says.

"My point is this," Padre says, "Yes, he's homeless, yes, he's panhandling. Maybe he's playing upon people's sympathies so they'll give him money. Does he deserve our condemnation because of that? What about having sympathy for his situation?"

"Damn, Padre, you aren't a priest. Realize that, will you?"

"I might not be a priest anymore, Wade, but I am not absolved of my responsibility to my fellow man. Neither are you."

"That's what I'm talking about," I say.

"You guys are just a couple of regular-ass goody-goodies," Wade says, "aren't you?"

"You are an unsympathetic person," Padre says. His second beer is gone. Well, fourth actually. Second of the ones he just brought back.

"I didn't say anything about sympathy. I'm saying the guy is working an angle. I don't like to have an angle worked on me. I'm not giving anything to anybody who works an angle on me."

"Like you've never worked an angle before," I say.

"I don't make my living working angles."

"Which of us has never worked an angle before, for a drink for example?" I say.

The minute those words are out of my mouth, it hits me like a drum beat inside my head that we really are alcoholics. I worked an angle on the bartender for the pitcher of beer in front of me right now. It was so easy. I'm getting flustered now and I say, "What's it say in the

Bible, Padre, 'He who does whatever shouldn't throw stones?'"

"Let he who is without sin cast the first stone."

"Don't cast stones, Wade. That's what I'm saying," I say.

"You are a retard," he says and finishes his beer. "I'm going up to the bar to get another one. I am going to use money to do it. I am going to use money that I earned working at an honest job. Nobody can hold that against me."

"It's day labor. It's not a job," I say.

"Yes, but I earned it honest."

He walks away through the people and up to the bar.

"Wade pisses me off sometimes," I say.

"He pisses me off, too. Sometimes," Padre says.

"Padre."

"Is 'piss' considered a swear word?"

"I don't think so."

"You might have made a good priest," Padre says.

"Really?" I say and for a second I feel honored.

"Something about this man in the wheelchair obviously touches something in you. Your compassion is triggered in some way. Priests are called to be compassionate."

"I don't think I could be a priest, though. My dad told me stories about Catholic school."

"Priests have gotten a bad reputation. Not a fair one, by and large. Most are good priests," Padre says.

I look at Padre. He is staring into his beer glass. There's an inch left in it. His eyes have gotten red. He puts the palm of his hand on his forehead and sighs.

"Well," he says, after a couple seconds.

"I think we're alcoholics, Padre," I say.

"I think you might be right," he says. He doesn't look at me.

"Did you ever, you know, counsel any alcoholics when you were a priest?" I say.

"A lot of them."

"What did you say?"

"Pray for God to take away your desire to drink." Padre is staring out the window.

"Did you ever pray that yourself?"

"Lots of times."

"Yeah, I was thinking I might pray something like that, too. Do you think God will do it?"

Padre looks at me. There is this look in his eyes, I can't quite tell what. Like he's mad or something.

"Didn't you hear what I just said?" Padre says.

"Yeah, Padre. You said you counseled alcoholics to pray for God to take away their desire to drink," I say.

"After that."

"That you prayed it, too."

"I said I prayed that prayer lots of times, Michael. For me. Many, many times. I prayed it right before I walked into this bar," Padre says. His grip on his glass has tightened. "I'm praying it right now."

"You're praying right now?" I say.

"Right now," Padre says.

"I didn't see you cross yourself."

"I didn't cross myself, Michael. I don't do that any more. I just pray. I just pray and pray. And you know what?" Padre is a little tipsy now, that's for sure.

"What?"

"Nothing ever happens, St. Michael the Archangel."

"Now, come on, Padre, don't talk like that." I want to put my arm around him and hold him close and tell him it's all going to be okay. I want to tell him, "Just have faith," but I don't really know if it's okay to tell an ex-priest that.

Wade comes back with a full glass. He takes a drink and some foam dissolves on his upper lip.

"Cubs fucked it up. They left two men on." Wade points to the TV. The Cubs are running out onto the field now. The game is close to being over. Wade plunks down in his chair and watches. Padre continues to look deep into his beer glass. I glance back and forth between the two of them. We are alcoholics. We were alcoholics, we are now alcoholics, and we will continue to be alcoholics, and I realize that I don't want to continue to be an alcoholic.

"I'm going to go talk to him," I say, "the guy in the wheelchair."

"You're what?" Wade says.

"I want to talk to him. I want to ask him some questions. No offense to you guys, but I don't want to sit here anymore." I stand up.

"Sit down. The game's almost over. There's a million people out there," Wade says.

"I don't care. I'm going. I'm going to talk to him. I'll see you guys," I say.

"Padre, what's this guy talking about?" Wade says, but Padre doesn't say anything.

I move toward the door and my legs feel a little weak. My head is swimming and I know I'm drunk. I move out into the bright afternoon sunshine. It's a beautiful day. The sidewalks are starting to fill up with people in their red and Cubbie blue. Girls with long blonde hair coming out from under their Cubs caps. Dudes with flip-flops and gray Cubs shirts or pinstriped jerseys and sunglasses and backward caps. The sunshine plays down on all of us, lights us all up, throws shadows from all of us of equal length. We are all attending to our business in some way. Trying to make it to the Red Line before it gets stuffed with the post-game crowd. Trying to find a taxi. Trying to get to the guy on Addison in the wheelchair. I head down Sheffield under the new bleachers and turn right at Addison by the Harry Cary. I weave through all the people hanging out at the Captain Morgan's they built for people who come to ballgames to not watch ballgames. The sidewalk gets really small, really tightly packed. There is the wall of the stadium on my right and the line of buses on Addison on my left and not much room to move in between. I can smell the heavy exhaust from all the buses and it makes my stomach turn a little. I keep pushing my way forward, shuffling along behind everybody else. Finally, I come to him.

He's plopped in the wheelchair and leaning to the left. He's kind of a big fat guy. He barely fits in the chair. The sun is baking his skin. He wears a Cubs hat and a ripped-up Cubs t-shirt and black tennis shoes that look like they came from the secondhand store. He's sunburned and the skin on his nose is blistered. He's got these bright blue eyes that stare without blinking. On his lap is the sign that says 'Please Help' in black marker. I stand right in front of him, and, like an idiot, I don't know what to say to start with. He rolls his eyes toward me.

"Hey," I say. "Sorry, I don't have any change."

The guy mumbles something.

"I didn't catch that." I lean in.

"Then don't block the people." His voice sounds like it's been baked in an oven. It's not much louder than a whisper.

I turn and see there's a jam-up of people behind me and I move so I'm standing next to the guy and out of everybody's way. The sun is beating down and I'm getting really hot. I catch a wave of BO from him.

"Are you really faking this?" I say.

His eyes dart right at me. They don't blink, even though the sun is beating down.

"I mean, my friend Wade says this is all a put-on but I say it's real," I say.

"What the fuck?" His voice is still low, but it's louder now and I can hear him.

"I didn't say that right," I say. I feel my stomach really start to churn now and the sweat is coming down my face. My head feels like it's coming apart. I got up from the table with Padre and Wade too fast.

"Get out of here," he says.

"Wait," I say. "Don't tell me that shit. I'm just trying to figure out if you really need the help or not. I'm saying, I think you do. I think you're really paralyzed and I don't think you're ripping people off at all."

"Motherfucker, of course I'm paralyzed," he says, and now his jaw is jutting out. I can see his bottom teeth.

"Just listen to me. I'm just trying to ask you some questions."

"Fuck off," he screeches. I mean, he really screeches it.

I notice a bunch of people are looking at us. Then the guy in the chair starts to move. He turns his body, like he's trying to force himself out of the chair. For a second, I think maybe he's faking the whole thing and he's about to stand up and beat the shit out of me. He pushes himself up with his one good foot on the ground. His body comes up a few inches out of the chair and I try to take a step back, but there's no place for me to go because of all the people. Then his good foot suddenly goes sliding out and since it had all his weight on it, he crashes back down into the chair. The chair rocks and squeaks and his body quivers. The side of him that's paralyzed flops around in this sick kind of way. Then he does all that again. He pushes himself up with his good foot and it flies out and he lands back in the chair. He does this again and then again, faster and faster, bouncing his giant body like it was a basketball. I swear I don't know how the chair is not collapsing.

"Look at me, motherfucker, look at me," he screams.

"Hey, man, calm down," I say. Everybody is staring now.

"I'm paralyzed, motherfucker. Paralyzed," he shouts. He is staring right at me while he bounces himself, faster and faster. I swear I have never seen anything like it and it scares the shit out of me, to tell the truth.

"I move like this, I move like this," he starts shouting.

I am about to pass out on the ground. He's yelling at me. He's taunting me. That giant body jerking around is freakish and grotesque and it's me he wants to see it.

"I move like this," he keeps shouting, as he bounces, his high-pitched voice piercing the rumble of the buses.

Everybody is staring at him. I mean, everybody. But it feels like they're staring at me, too. The guy is staring right at me.

"I don't know this motherfucker," I mumble.

I force myself into the stream of people. Some lady calls me a name as I cut in front of her, but I don't care, I just want the hell away from that fucking mutant. I push my way through the crowd until the space widens out up closer to Clark. I hear the guy's voice, and I'm not sure if it's real or in my mind, but I definitely hear it. I dart through some of the open spaces between the people and make my way north on Clark to Waveland and then hang a right, back toward Murphy's. I didn't realize how fast my heart was beating and now it feels like it's about to hammer its way out of my chest. Big thudding beats. I'm sucking in gasps of air and I stop and lean on the wall of Wrigley underneath the bleachers and catch my breath. It takes a long time.

When I finally calm down, I go back into Murphy's. The place is emptier now. The ballgame has ended. The Cubs lose. Wade is sitting at the same table by himself. He's got another one, half-gone, in front of him. Padre isn't there.

"Where's Padre?" I say.

"He left," Wade says.

I wish Padre was still there.

"Did you see the guy?"

"Yeah," I say, "I saw him."

"Did you give him some change?" Wade says.

"No." That's all I want to say.

"Well, what the hell did you talk to him about?" Wade says.

"Nothing. Not much. I just, you know, asked him if he needed anything," I say. I feel a touch of guilt and shame.

"Yeah? Did he need anything?" Wade says.

"You know, he just said he wanted something cold to

drink. He went to try to get some change out, but, you know, it's hard for him to move, so I said, 'Don't worry about it,' and I just ran across the street to Seven Eleven and got him a Gatorade."

"You bought him a Gatorade," Wade says.

"Yeah, I bought him a Gatorade," I say.

"But you never buy me a round," Wade says and holds up his glass.

I think about the guy jumping around in his chair. I think I'll see that in my mind for the rest of my life. I fight back a shudder.

"That's because you're a bastard," I say.

"Don't talk like that to me," Wade says. "I'm not a bastard. Fuck you."

12 WAR

We pounded the hills. We pounded the shoulders of the mountains. There were orange blooms of flame among the boulders and fir trees and high stalks of smoke rising and blowing slowly off. The guns boomed and boomed and boomed, with deep echoes rolling away down the valleys. We pounded them from sun-up to sundown. We pounded them all through the night. We pounded them in shifts, ragged men returning mud-caked from the guns, reporting to their replacements: "The bastards are on the run now. We've got them where we want them now. Give 'em hell now," and so forth. We pounded them through breakfast, lunch, and supper, teatime too, and through the afternoon siesta if you observed it like the Spaniards did. We pounded them until we believed it was possible through guts and guts alone to make a rough place plain.

Then, one afternoon in late fall, the cranes came. Drifting high on updrafts, flying in single-file squadrons, slipping into the blue smoke on the wind, cat-cat-cattering in arrhythmic squawks, they descended into our lines of site and the guns went quiet. The cranes weren't quiet, though. Their chirruping sounded like machine-gun bursts. And worst was the raw throated screams they emitted—a sound with power enough to shatter our spines as we hunkered under the guns. Finally we all plugged our ears with mud and sticks and waited, and three days later the cranes had all flown off down the valleys.

Nothing was left then. We turned our eyes to the mountaintops, gold in the setting sun, the color burning down to auburn then azure as the sun disappeared, and through the night and through the week and weeks to come we heard nothing but the Captain's voice, from time to time, issuing toothless orders.

"Shine those barrels, boys. Clean the mud from the gearboxes. Dry the caissons again. Dry them again, I said. Again."

13 THE GOD OF THE LIVING ROOM

I'm at Tom's apartment staring at the big deer head he has hanging on the wall of his living room. Tom has a small place and the deer head looks enormous. Some kind of giant, mutant deer, like it's god of the living room. It's mounted over the couch, so when you sit down to watch TV it probably feels like the deer is watching TV over your shoulder.

"Where did you get this thing?" I say.

Tom is in the kitchen cooking up some bacon and eggs for dinner for the two of us. He and his wife are separated and I wonder if he eats bacon and eggs every night.

"I shot him."

"No shit," I say.

I met Tom at the Twelve Step House. Three months ago I'd showed up drunk as hell and blubbering for help. Really crying. I'm not ashamed of that, of the crying. To tell the truth, the night I washed up on the Twelve Step House's porch I was homeless. Homeless! I'd drank myself out of my indie barista job downtown, then out of my apartment, then out of friends' places, then ended up in a shelter—a human warehouse—on the West Side, getting picked clean by bedbugs every night. It was Tom who poured me some of that awful coffee from the ancient silver urn that sits there in the common room and never seems to be off. He agreed to sponsor me after I kept showing up for the meetings. I was supposed to meet Tom out for coffee tonight, actually, but I had an emergency at work and couldn't make it to the coffee shop before it closed. I just got hired on as a route driver for this vending machine company. Some Board of Trade type got his Snickers bar stuck in a coil and I had to go set it free.

"After you shoot a deer, you have to dress it out. Gut it." Tom is wiping his hands on a grimy towel that has these little faded flowers printed along the edge.

"I bet that's disgusting," I say.

"You take this special field-dressing knife, start at the deer's anus, and cut through his gut. Rip him open right up to his neck."

"Anus?"

"You have to stick your hand in there to hold the carcass down while you slice."

"That's nasty."

"There was venison in the house for a year after that little excursion." Tom points to the deer head with the spatula.

He shows me where the plates and silverware are and tells me to set the table while he finishes cooking up the bacon and eggs. I can't remember the last time I actually set a table, so it kind of amuses me. I get out the juice and find these little juice cups, about a million of them, all stacked neatly way in the back of the cupboard. In a few minutes, Tom has the bacon and eggs on our plates and we sit down.

"Will you bless the food, Joey?" he says.

My fork is already hovering above my plate.

"I'll do it," he says.

Tom starts to talk out loud to God, and so I point my head down, but I peek at him. His big wrinkly hands are folded, eyes closed tightly, bushy eyebrows scrunched to-gether like a couple of wrecked caterpillars. He closes with the Serenity Prayer, and I mutter along because I at least know the words to that one now. We amen together.

"Dig in," Tom says.

So I do. I'm hungry. For awhile, Tom and I just sit and eat and don't say anything. When our plates are mostly empty, he wipes his mouth with the back of his hand. He has a white mustache and a scraggly goatee and there are some bits of scrambled egg stuck in it at the corners of his mouth. It's kind of disgusting. I heard somebody say once that alcoholics are perpetually on the path back to civiliz-ation, but they can't ever really get there.

"Do you pray much?" Tom says.

I pause with a final pasty wad of food in my mouth. Tom is sitting back in his chair, arms folded now.

"Well, do you pray at all?" he says.

I swish some coffee through my teeth and say, "No, Tom. No, I really don't."

Tom drums his crooked fingers on the table and stands up. "Done?" He points to my plate. I nod. He whisks both our plates away and I hear them crash-land into the sink. I follow him into the little kitchen, but he doesn't turn around. He starts washing the plates and sil-verware by hand. No dishwasher.

"I used to pray," I say. "I used to go to mass. I had this wooden rosary I got at confirmation, but I have no idea where it is now."

"Dry these dishes, will you?" Tom tosses me a towel, the same grimy, flowery one he was wiping his hands on while he cooked. I make a little game of it, trying to grab the dish, dry it, and put it back in the cupboard before Tom can finish washing the next one and set it in the dry-ing rack. Eventually, there are no more dishes.

"You are aware, of course, that recovery involves a Higher Power, as we say?" Tom says, shaking soapy drips from his hands.

"I know."

"If you don't pray, my dear boy, how exactly do you plan to communicate with this Higher Power?"

I puff out my cheeks and shrug my shoulders. What a weird question.

"Show me how you prayed," Tom says.

"What?"

"How did you pray, the last time you prayed?"

"How should I know," and I was about to say something else, but Tom interrupts.

"Was it this?" he says, and makes a giant, elaborate sign of the cross on his chest, real big, his hand flopping up and down, and side to side through the motions.

"Yeah, something like that." I'm standing with my hands in my pockets and I eye the front door.

"Come on, come in here," he says, and points to the living room, away from the door.

I go, hands still in my pockets. "What?" I say.

Then Tom kneels down in front of the couch. He's kind of an old guy, so he has to kneel balancing against the couch's arm, one leg at a time. His joints pop. I hear him grunt a little under his breath and when that first knee clonks on the floor his eyes pop wide, all that loose skin in his cheeks seizing up just for a second. I have no idea what he's doing.

"Let us pray," he says, his voice a grimace.

"Pray?"

"That's right. Now, kneel down here beside me."

I think he looks ridiculous.

"Pray to what, to the deer?"

Tom looks up at it, smiles, and then says, "Sure."

I snort a little laugh. "I don't think God would appreciate that."

"How do you know what God appreciates?" Tom says. "Will you join me?"

I stare at him for a long time.

"This is weird." I shake my head.

Tom looks up at the deer and then at his hands folded in front of him. His body compresses a little as he exhales a big breath. Then he gets to his feet.

"Working tomorrow?" he says.

"Bright and early."

"Okay. Well, I'm going to bed," Tom says. "You can let yourself out. Lock the knob, would you?"

He disappears into his bedroom and after a few minutes, the skinny, horizontal line of pale light coming from underneath his door turns black.

"Well, then," I say, "goodnight to you, too," and then I head for the front door. I have my hand on the doorknob when I look back at the deer head and say, "Have a good night, deer head." Its yellow eyes are huge, wide open, giving it a look of surprise. It's the same look it must have had on its face the instant the bullet ripped through its body, shredding its heart and lungs and liver.

"Tough stuff being a deer, huh?" I say to it. My hand falls off the doorknob.

I was never a hunter, and suddenly I want to touch it. I walk over, step up on the couch and put a hand on its nose. It's rough like tiny pebbles, but I imagine it was once cold and wet, like a dog's nose. I rub the coarse hair on the neck and pinch the knobby antlers between my thumb and forefinger. And I never knew this: deer have eyelashes.

"Okay," I say. "Okay."

I smile a little. A twitch of my lips, really.

"Deer," I say, "I want to be sober."

Now I see that the deer is looking out beyond me, out into the shadows of Tom's apartment. Then I feel the deer's gaze. Feel it suddenly looking at me. I suck in a little breath, find myself actually bowing my head, and even though I'm thinking, 'What the hell are you doing?' I still do it. I let it look at what I have been as it considers every glass of beer I've ever poured down my throat, every bottle of whiskey, knowing even the time I drank the mouthwash at the dentist's office years ago. Because, I suppose, of some need I feel to make the atmosphere more sacred, I yank the pull-cord on the light on the ceiling fan and now, in the dark of Tom's living room, there is a hazy shine, a mellow golden color, on the antlers from the streetlight outside. They are a crown. I kneel. More sound comes out of me. My lips move but I'm not sure if it's me talking willfully or if the deer is siphoning words out of my soul, words that describe things I've only ever thought but buried, and recollections of my dark sins, the really black ones. And then wishes pour out of me, spilling onto the couch like blood from a bull on an altar. Big wishes for the whole of humanity—world peace and things like that—then, medium wishes—a better job, a wife, kids even, which I've never, ever wanted before, and even small wishes I laugh at but still mean—the Cubs in the Series, for example. I wish to hate booze, wish that my stomach would catch fire and burn me to death from the inside out if I ever take another drink. I wish for a better life, for a new me, for a better spirit. Without knowing exactly what that means, I wish for a better spirit. When I get done with all the wishing, I'm exhausted, a kind of exhaustion I've never felt before. Like I've been vacuumed out or like each piece of my guts has been removed, dunked in a bucket, dried on a line, and stuck back inside me. I can't think another thought. Then the room starts to go dark. Not nighttime darkness, but final darkness type shit, an Armageddon thing. Then the thought pops into my head: 'My god...it's chosen to end the world,' but I don't panic. Any fear I have, or even ever had, is absorbed into a blue-colored peace, which is the direction I head when my eyes go closed, when the lights finally go out. But a few minutes later, what seems like a few minutes later at least, I feel a warm, gentle pressure on my shoulder and I pop my eyes open. Sunlight fills the living room. Tom, standing above me, is squeezing my shoulder.

"Wake up, Joey," he is saying. "It's morning. You're going to be late."

14 THE WHEELCHAIR BEAUTY

Monday night I was sitting at the coffee shop—*my* coffee shop, as I've come to call it, though it's actually called, somewhat tongue-in-cheekily, Mama Earth's. (Everything now is tongue in cheek, isn't it?) I was sipping something South American, I think—it had citrus notes—and reading Fitzgerald. I've already read all of his short stories, and am now working my way through his novels, starting with everybody's favorite, *The Great Gatsby*. Hemingway was before Fitzgerald, Dos Passos before Hemingway. (Look, Ma! I'm the Lost Generation!) At some point, I happened to glance up and saw through the window, approaching *my* coffee shop, three young people. Hipsters. A woman/girl, a man/boy, and another woman/girl nearly identical to the first, except that she was in a wheelchair. Sisters, maybe twins. But Mama Earth's has no wheelchair ramp. There is only a small step from the sidewalk to the door, so the ambulatory female held the door open (some clever Mama Earth's staffer had rigged a door chime which tinkled through the opening riff of the Pixies' "Where is My Mind?") and the man/boy tipped the bound girl back, then up, then over the step, and shoved her inside. They took a table near me. All three of them acted like it was nothing.

The girl in the wheelchair sat straight-backed, hands folded in her lap. What was wrong with her? No white plaster casts, her legs were firm, shapely even—this I could see through the faded indigo fabric of her jeans, which conformed to every ripple of her flesh. She had neither the telltale turned-in toes nor the muscular atrophy of somebody with a more serious condition. I don't doubt that she needed a wheelchair, mind you. All I mean to say is that whatever her malady, the necessity of a wheelchair was not evident to me.

The man/boy began a conversation with some droll line at which they all laughed, including himself, perhaps he the hardest. I could not make out what it was, but I'd imagine it was something slathered in irony. As soon as the laughter died down, he arose and went to the counter, returning with three cups of coffee. I tried to get back to my book.

The woman/girl in the wheelchair sat facing me. Her sister (I presumed) sat to her right, in profile to me, and the man/boy to her left. His profile included a gentle slope from protruding lower lip all the way down to his Adam's apple. Essentially, he was chinless. Once, when he frowned, I saw a slight bump in the line, the nascent hump of a chin, but it disappeared as soon as his countenance changed. I saw a future for him, and it did not look good. Perhaps, if he were lucky, he'd be the last proprietor of a thing already on its way out: the independent bookstore. Likely named The Naked Eye, Alternative Pages, or some such gobbledygook. Maybe Gobbledygook would be the name of it. "Please, sir, buy a book. Buy a book for the poor, please, sir?" Yes, that was him. Or would be.

The sister, the one who could walk, was probably twenty years old, maybe twenty-one, but she held her face all wrong. It appeared that inside of her head, just under the thin layer of fairly pretty skin, were the muscles and skull of a mean old woman who controlled the girl's face and was intentionally misusing it. There were far too many wrinkles around her lips—from too much smoking already? Too much ironic smiling? (To smile ironically, one simply purses one's lips as hard as one can possibly purse them. That's it. And this is what it means: "Love me, I hate you, love me, make me laugh, make me laugh NOW damn you. I hate you." Ah, the banter of love. What a racket.)

The wheelchair woman looked at both of her companions, bright eyes darting back and forth, back and forth. They seemed to amuse her, these friends or family or whoever they were. She didn't say much, though clearly understood all, and she never spoke first. Every now and then, her eyes turned toward the ceiling, brief little glances that I'm sure only I saw. Had she noticed the brown blooms of water stains in the drop ceiling panels and did they disturb her? Maybe she saw immaculate angels climbing to heaven. If she could climb, would she have climbed to heaven with them? And once, her eyes met mine, a demure glance, but surely not an invitation. They'd only just gotten here! Her mouth was a delicate plum. The lips were smooth and evenly wetted, with glints of light like blazing cat scratches upon the lower one. Her smile forced her freckled skin back in little mounds over her high cheekbones. And there were dimples. Two of them.

I forced my eyes down, back to my book, but could not keep them there for more than a paragraph, a few lines of dialogue. Eventually, my eyes could not stay on the page for the length of time it takes to read a comma or a period. So I pretended. When she spoke, she often touched her fingertips to her white cheeks, both cheeks sometimes. When she laughed, it was a high-pitched giggle tinged with a just so perfect amount of womanly remorse. She talked and laughed and nodded and on and on like a little geisha flapper girl and the sound of her laughing and talking rose from the table like a bunch of multicolored balloons.

Perhaps I fell in love.

I really don't know how much time passed, but it can

be measured in two ways: Since she and her party had entered Mama Earth's I'd read a total of one half of one page. Obviously, that should just take seconds. "I wasn't actually in love, but I felt a sort of tender curiosity." And why not? When I first saw her, I'd admitted to myself that she was beautiful, something many men could not do, would not do.

But suddenly, it seemed they had completed their business, whatever that business was, even if that business was simply weighing down the chairs. That was, of course, the business of her friends. Her business, it seemed, was to enchant me. Their conversations were finished. Their cups of coffee (and each with a refill) drained. This was the second way, an anomaly of time, the passing of it literally as on the faces of clocks, but oh how the faces of the beautiful spin the hands of clocks with unnatural speed! Her friends stood. My girl stood in her spirit, much taller.

Her friends moved toward the exit, but she, finding a convenient bypass to an array of splayed chairs from another nearby table, wheeled around and found her path to the door, which led directly in front of my table.

"Goodnight," I risked.

She stopped and looked at me.

"What?" she said.

"Just goodnight." I could not help it, my smile, so wide.

She stared at me and my heart soared.

"Why are you—" Her voice trailed off.

"Pardon?"

"Did you just tell me goodnight?" she asked.

"Yes." I could barely even say this tiny little word.

"Uh, goodnight? I guess?" she said, and then was gone, wheeling to the door and over and down the step by herself, a clattering bump, her companions trailing after her. The boy, the book-monger, glanced over his shoulder at me, his best attempt at a withering glare a misfire. It was the pained look one wears at the height of a calamity in the bowels. So I swallowed the dregs from my mug. I didn't—couldn't—return to my book, so until the man/boy (another one) at the counter announced, "Ten minutes until closing," I watched a girl dressed in black drawing with children's markers in a Hello Kitty notebook.

15 GOING TO MESA WITH HENRY

This was last summer I met a guy called Henry. He threw me a little scratch to drive with him out to his ex-lady's house. It had been their house, he said, but after they went splitsville she wound up with all the good stuff. Henry wound up my neighbor at a motel in the sketchy part of town, around Van Buren and 10th Avenue, down by all the soup lines. Matter of fact, all he got in the final deal was the bitty little Honda we were riding in. I think he spent some time living in it, before the motel. When they were together, him and his lady, they'd lived out in Mesa and had some good times. Mesa, where we were heading to. A nice place. They had kids. I think he said a son, maybe two sons, maybe a daughter. He said it had been ages since he talked to either them or his ex-lady.

"So, wait, what are we doing?" I asked. The tires whined on the 202 below us, loud as an industrial AC unit. Henry was hunched up over the steering wheel. He gave me a giddy, sideways look, eyes wide. Licking his lips. Then he said, "I'm so glad you made the decision to come along with me. It was the right decision. Helping out a friend. We're friends, and you help out your friends."

"Sure," I said.

Henry whapped my arm and, instinctively, I made a muscle. That made me smile, that instant tension in my bi, like a steel cable, I pictured, lifting a long I-beam into the brains of some new building. They were always putting up new buildings. Steel and glass monsters looming up out of the desert. Or maybe it was I smiled because Henry paid attention. Paid me some attention anyway.

"But, wait though, what?" I said.

"Take a look in the back seat there." Henry threw a thumb over his shoulder.

There were a bunch of coins down on the floorboards, and an old blue-handled toothbrush, too. On the ripped-up seat sat a burlap sack, half-open.

"What's in it?" I said.

"Go on, open it, open it." Henry was watching me instead of the road, so we cruised right onto the shoulder and nearly flew out into the desert, before Henry whipped the wheel around and got us back onto the highway. We made an awful skidding, screeching racket. Made my face bang into his seat and I chomped my lip.

"Damn it."

"Seatbelts," Henry screamed. "Seatbelts!"

I flipped the burlap sack all the way open and inside were crowbars, a couple of hammers, tin snips, all brand new. Still had barcodes on them, Home Depot stickers, too.

"Looks like you got some hardware here," I said, still leaning into the back.

"Uh-huh!" Henry was excited.

"Oh, I get it," I said. "We're going to rip her place off. Right?"

"No," he said, "better."

"Better?"

"You don't see any ski masks back there, do you? Gloves?"

"No."

"We're going to rip her place UP!" he cackled.

I plonked down in the passenger seat, coughing on the little dust cloud that'd brewed in the air from my wide ass bouncing around. Way up above us were the last rays of the sun, orange forks across this azure sky, tines going every which way. I swear, from one side of the sky to another. And behind those, you could just start to see little dots of stars, like we were under the skin of heaven and God kept shoving a needle through, looking for a vein, looking for lifeblood. Heaven burned on the other side. And there I sat with Henry.

"How big's the house?" I said.

"Not big. Not big." Henry's head bobbed and his bony fingers wouldn't be still on the steering wheel, like it was a circular piano he was trying to play.

"Are you lit?" I said.

"Nope."

We were quiet.

"Maybe," he said then, "but only a little bit."

So, yeah, we made it out to Mesa. Henry couldn't find the ex-old-lady's house, even though it used to be his house. We drove up and down streets that all looked the same, with low squatty houses supposed to look like haciendas. He kept saying, "I think this is it," or "No, this one here," until we were both totally turned around bass-ackwards. He pulled the car onto the shoulder after we'd looped around probably the hundredth cul-de-sac, killed the headlights, and started to cry. Big sucking sobs. I didn't know what the hell to do. After a few minutes he calmed down. His crying became wheezing, became sighs, became little murmurs of breath, these tiny putters of air I'd never heard come from any man's mouth before. They were delicate. Like they could pop.

"Are you okay, Henry?" I said.

"Yes. No. I don't know."

"What do you say we head back?"

Henry let his head fall onto his hand. He rubbed his face and I could hear his beard stubble scratching on his open palm. He stared out of the window for a long time. Then he said, "No, let's wait. This one might be the street. Maybe she'll recognize the car."

16 THE WRECK OF THE FREDERICK W. DANBY

I.

The freighter tears apart and men fall into the breach. There goes Costigan, now Bobek, and now the Williams brothers. They'll be crushed, or drowned, and either way buried in the silt at the bottom of the lake. The taconite from the holds will go right down on top of them.

This is a dream. Please.

II.

Burke is curled up like a shrimp in the stern of the lifeboat and in the bow another man lies tangled in a white wool blanket. Trough to crest, trough to crest, the boat rides the waves and the wind is merciless, skinning the water alive and flinging star-sparkling pelts on board the little boat.

Neither man moves.

III.

In a sort of vision, Burke sees a woman on the water walking toward him. He cannot remember where he is or why he is there, but he is on the water. He does know that. But maybe that's only because he has been on the water ever since he was born, his blood transfused now, so that what pumps through even his tiniest capillary is the ancient water of the Great Lakes. Coal, ice, limestone, ore: his body parts. The woman says she is his wife, with long brown hair, but she's not his wife. She misses him. Please come home, she says. Don't you miss me?

IV.

Burke is shocked awake. He bangs his head on the underside of a thwart and the blood runs into his eye. Lake Superior in all directions to infinite horizons. Blue sky above and the sun a bright hole, but all is frigid and the wind moves over the boat like a charging moose. He tucks below the gunwale. Up front is a white woolen pile with one white-socked foot protruding, and the wind flapping the blanket so hard it cracks in a rhythm. He finds his knees have frozen and he cannot crawl or stand, so he grabs his pea coat tight at the collar and shoves out the words, feeling his Adam's apple bob against his knuckles.

"Hey in the bow."

Burke clenches his jaw until his teeth grit, tightens all the muscles he can feel, then flops his body over the thwart. He clunks onto the floor and, landing in the pool at the bottom, gasps, then splashes up and over the next thwart, then the next until he is beside the pile of blankets. Burke peels them back until he finds a gray face—but both eyes are purple plum-like mounds with crooked incisions for eye slits. Burke shakes him. It's Torres, a Mexican, one of the *Danby's* oilers. And he isn't dead. Torres counted on another Mexican and a Puerto Rican to speak, listen, and tell.

"Are you okay?" Burke shouts anyway.

Torres rolls his head away so he is facing the sky.

V.

How many men were on board? Thirty whatever it was. Must be in 500, 600 feet of water. Probably 600 feet. 600 feet. They know about us by now in the Sault and we'll see choppers anytime. Wouldn't be surprised if we wash up on shore somewhere before they have a chance to find us. Hope it ain't Canadian shores. Damn boat sunk and fuck me sideways if I didn't grab my passport before I got off.

VI.

"I'm getting under there with you," Burke says. "Me and you are going to spoon like high-school sweethearts."

Torres groans and stirs, the blanket shifting like skin with a worm underneath. His mouth is pulled down at the corners in a frozen and flat-lipped grimace.

"For both of us," Burke says. "We have to. I know you don't know what the hell I'm saying."

Burke maneuvers his body against Torres', tugs at the blanket and starts to heave himself beneath, but he feels Torres' arm stiffen with more strength than he imagined Torres had, feels the arm pushing into his belly. From Torres' still tightened jaw, half-words in Spanish come hissing out with great, wasted pressure behind them so his speech sounds like a broken boiler popping with consonants.

"No hablo español, amigo," Burke says, and Torres screeches, a high whine that peters out in the cold and falls plinking into the boat.

"You worried I ain't going to kiss you goodnight? No besos?" Burke says. "I'll buy you dinner when we get back on land."

Torres hammers his fist into Burke's gut.

"Asshole—" Burke starts, but looking down between their bodies, he sees a dark pool on the floorboards of the lifeboat. Burke scrambles back. Torres' slicker has been sheared away and a long slash runs from Torres' upward-facing left side, traversing his back, and disappears under his downward-facing right side. The white of the backbone peeks through the cut as it widens and pinches shut with the rocking of the boat.

VII.

In the night, there are more stars than he has ever seen before, maybe more than any man has ever seen. With light so bright that it casts shadows. Burke moves his hand over the white blanket and watches a black hand wave back. And he thinks about Indians and Indian raiders and broad-bladed flint knives with thigh-bone handles. Then about dead animals, carcasses half-buried in the leaves with antlers like pitted spindles sprouting from the forest floor. He is in the forest, then. There is nothing to eat and nothing to drink, so he crawls into a deerskin, licks lichen and the salty minerals oozing from sandstone boulders and becomes a deer and lives.

VIII.

Burke checks Torres, whose chest is rising and falling still, barely. He unhitches the belt, his own belt that he'd looped around Torres' belly and which he'd used to bind his own wadded-up Henley against the gash. Burke squeezes out blood into the lake, shakes the shirt, and then rebinds it to

Torres. Then Burke sits on the gunwale, unlaces his boot, and pulls off his wool sock. His foot is white, all the toes stuck together, and he cannot feel any of them. He dips the sock in the lake and rings it out, dips it and rings it out, dips it again, but this time doesn't ring it out. He hobbles one-footed to Torres and holds the sock above Torres' mouth.

"Agua," Burke says, and squeezes the sock so a bead of the freezing, clear water falls onto Torres' lips. Torres' tongue peeps out, flicks at the drops of water, then slips back inside his mouth.

"Mas," Burke says and squeezes the sock again. This time Torres opens his mouth and the water goes in and does not come out.

"Good. Bueno."

X.

"Bring me a fish, lake. A nice, big muskie. I'm starving. Let him jump right into this boat. And then let it rain fire, the kind that doesn't burn up little boats. And a doc for Torres here. He's in bad shape."

XI.

Just before the sun is finally drawn into the lake and the lake swallows up every lick of its fire, the woman returns, this time hovering above the lifeboat.

"Now where have you been?" Burke laughs.

She says she's been there the entire time.

"Well, how come I haven't seen you the entire time?"

Sometimes she can't be seen.

"Because you're a hallucination of mine."

The woman's eyes roll back. She opens her mouth and then her throat erupts with a swarm of tiny orange and white helicopters, mini Jayhawk choppers like the Coast Guard uses. They fly at his eyes, nose, mouth, ears. He swats them, yells, covers his face, ducks turtle-like into his pea-coat collar, and when the silence returns they're gone. She's gone.

XII.

Torres dies. Sometime when the sun is highest—a day or two or a decade or two after the wreck—his heart just quits. Alive and dead, he looks the same. Who do we tell and how do we tell them? Burke reclaims the belt, the Henley, the sock. The belt he loops back around his own hips and he lays out the shirt and sock in the sun and has to keep banging the granules of ice off. When his patience is gone he puts them back on, the sock first, then the Henley.

Does the body stay? In the prow like a figurehead? Or does it get wrapped in the blanket and shoved off into the lake? Torres is Mexican, so does that mean Catholic, too? Burke says half an Our Father, forgets the words, starts over, comes to "on earth as it is in Heaven," and can't remember anymore.

XIII.

It's not necessarily sleep he drifts into and out of—more like he keeps floating between two dimensions. Blown between them—one of cold and ice, brilliant light and brilliant dark, now death, too, never-ending water in a boat pointed everywhere and nowhere all at once. The other much more uncertain—warmer, unreal. So, when he sits up one night after Torres dies, the boat still rocks in the water, but next to the corpse he sees a fish and a deer and the fish speaks: "Let's eat him."

"Who?" Burke croaks. "Me?"

They ignore him. The fish unhinges its jaws, swallows Torres, and snaps its jaws shut, a little tail of white wool blanket hanging from the jaws' V. The deer bends over and out shoots its pink tongue with machine-gun rapidity on the gunwale, licking, licking, licking up all the metal until the boat is nude the boat drifts apart in pieces the boat spreads out generously on the lake.

"Me too," Burke croaks. "Eat me, too!"

17 INCENDIARY

I think the social worker was supposed to come check on me from time to time, because I was seventeen, but all he did was drop me off at Uncle Lester's, and I never saw him again.

Lester was tall, skinny, and stooped, like me I guess, and went in and out of rooms at a shuffle, ducking door frames even when he didn't need to. He smelled like half-tanned cow hide, but looking back, that was the chemicals. Had to have been. That first night at the dinner table, just me and him in the farmhouse kitchen, sitting under a busted light fixture. Plates of frozen peas and Spam fried up with Crisco in front of us. Lester made no bones to me about who he was or what he did.

"Look, son, just so's you understand, I make and sell illegal drugs."

"Yessir."

"From time to time, you'll see different vehicles pull up. That'll be customers. You point them in my direction and don't say nothing. You can't tell how some of the more twitchy ones is gonna respond to a stranger. They're all packing heat, every last one of them."

"Yessir."

"This ain't a family business, son, but the farming is. Or was. Come sun-up, you'll see that I ain't maintained the fields. This other business I do, it takes up all my time now and I ain't got no help."

"You want me to help?" I said.

"Too eager. Cool your heels around here a while and we'll see. Meantime, you just stay out of the way. You got the notion though you could get the farm back in order. Hate to see the land go to waste."

"What, like, plow it?"

"That's one thing," he said and chewed his Spam and washed it down with beer from a jar, stood up and disappeared upstairs. I listened to him stump around until I figured he was in bed, and then I stretched out on the couch in the living room and conked out—my first night in the brand new place.

Lester was regular as a bowel movement with his work. He was up early every morning, weekends, too, way before I got up. I'd find his fresh boot prints in the little muddy trace from the kitchen door to the big barn behind the house. From between the barn wall slats, especially late in the evening, I'd catch flickers of orange, sometimes yellow and bright white flashes and every now and then it'd go suddenly, completely black. That's when I'd hear Lester faintly, like a whisper on the wind, god-damning pretty much everything in the known universe. And it was true what he said: People were always wheeling up the drive in rust-bucket pickup trucks, slipping into the barn to see him and then bouncing back out down the drive.

I watched these people. Bug-eyed freaks with shocks of gray or white hair most of them. Most of them men and lots of them with a woman waiting in the passenger seat, banging on the dashboard, the windshield, the roof, flapping like a plugged chickenhawk when she'd spy her man coming back. Once, a guy pulled up bare-ass naked. Got out of his truck, popped a squat right there beside it and took a shit in the yard. Stood up, went to see Lester, came back and drove off like it was nothing. He didn't even wipe his ass. I screamed with laughter.

All that is to say, Lester left me pretty well alone and I left him pretty well alone. We usually ate dinner together in the kitchen, though. TV dinners, Hamburger Helper, spaghetti. Typically, we didn't say much, and Lester always looked like he was concentrating real hard on the Formica tabletop. One time I spoke up, though.

"You ever hear from my daddy?" I asked. My voice didn't sound like my voice for some reason. It was far away, hollow, and I wasn't sure that I actually wanted an answer, to tell the truth. The question just popped out of me. Lester munched his food, wiped his mouth with the back of his sleeve and sat back. His eyes, black shining things, shone on me and I looked down at my fingers and, for a second, was sorry I spoke up.

Finally, he just said, "Nope."

"Wonder where he's at."

"You and me both."

"Where do you think?"

Lester sat forward and went back to staring at the table. "Jail maybe."

I tried to laugh. "Yeah. Probably." And I should have left it at that, but I went ahead and kept on. I said, "If it's jail, what do you figure for?"

Lester dead-eyed me again and said, "Murder," like it was his own son maybe that Daddy had murdered.

"Murder? Really?"

His face softened. "Well, don't let me feed you horseshit, son. Hell if I know what for. Hell, that's if he's in jail. Maybe he ain't. Maybe he's got hisself another little family way out in some other state and living like a king."

Anyway, about the chicken coop. One afternoon, two weeks after I showed up, I was bored as hell. I'd tried to do like Lester said, to get the farm in order. It didn't take but a couple days to realize that wasn't going to happen, or if it was, it wasn't going to happen by my hand. For one thing, Lester didn't let me into the barn. That's where the tractor was. Plows, too, and pretty much everything else. I could drive a tractor. I had plenty of experience driving a tractor. Even knew how to fix 'em up—change the oil and other basics. But even if he did let me back in there, I'm sure the keys to it were long gone. And there weren't any animals to take care of and I don't count his scraggly damn dog. Only farm I ever heard of with no cows, no horses, no pigs. No chickens.

So, I was poking around the place and ended up by the coop. Who knows how long it had been since it last held chickens. It had a low roof that came up to my elbows covered with real roofing shingles, about half of which had slid off into decomposing piles in the overgrown grass. The roof had a couple of holes in it, wet-rotted clear through. Probably about to cave in completely. The ramp the chickens used to walk up and down to and from the little pen up in front had either collapsed or somebody'd stomped it down. It lay there caked with mud, sticking out like the little building's half-decayed tongue. It's a good question where the hell all the chickens went, but given the attention Lester paid to everything else around his place, they liked to have starved to death. That or carried off into the woods by coyotes. If that little coop was home, the chickens, what was left of 'em, were probably slathering themselves in barbecue sauce and begging the coyotes to drag 'em off.

I stooped to look inside and saw it was filled with what was surely some of Lester's old equipment. Empty gallon jugs piled up and some PVC pipe. Thick, hazy tubing like albino snakes. Stacks of what looked like the grates off the back of a refrigerator. I had no guess what he used those for. And as I gazed at that old stuff, there came over me a particular notion: I wondered what that old coop would look like wrapped up in flames. Black smoke peeling off, the way it pulses in evil coils up into a clear morning or a clear night. Making something and then letting it get away from you. It must be what God felt like way back at the beginning of time.

I yanked a piece of tubing from the pile and grabbed a jug and trotted over to Lester's truck—he was wrapped up in his work and wouldn't see me—and siphoned off some of the gas. Found me a half book of matches in the glove box. Zipped back to the coop. I had a boner. Hadn't been that hard since I swiped a Playboy from the gas station around the corner from my mother's house. This one surprised me, though.

Sloshed the gas all over the coop so by the time I was done, it was dripping down through the roof holes like it had flat out rained gas on the thing. Then I struck a match and held it to the flap of the matchbook and just for two seconds I watched the book curl up and turn brown in the little flame. Then I flung it onto the coop. In that same split second, I turned and bolted. Only got a step before— Whoom! I spun around and backpedaled, backpedaled, the suddenness of the heat shoving me through the uncut grass still damp with dew at the roots, shoving me until I fell on my ass, legs V-d out in front of me, and between them I watched the fire engulf the coop, turn the whole thing bright and orange and raging, watched it puke up big hunks of embers that spiraled and fell and for a long time there was only fire only fire and when the coop was just about consumed after who the hell knew how long and the flames shrunk down and I could see the building's black bones, I laid my head back in the sweet grass and went to sleep.

No clue how long I'd been out when I opened my eyes and discovered I was moving—sliding backward, watching my boot toes bump up and down over the divots in the yard. Somebody was pulling me by my armpits. I tossed my head back and twisted my shoulders and jumped-ed to my feet. Uncle Lester.

"You okay?" he said.

I looked at myself. The front of my shirt was speckled

with little cracked holes rimmed in black. Cinder burns. I put my hands on my face, blinked my eyes, stretched my arms out.

"I swear to you I didn't even hear it blow," he said.

I realized I was panting.

"I store cook shit in there. Old fumes must have combusted somehow." He was panting, too, hands on his knees, and he pointed a crooked finger at the remnant of the coop.

"You wasn't smoking near here was you?"

I shook my head. "I don't smoke."

"You sure you're okay?"

I nodded and Lester let out a chuckle.

"Probably scared the hell out of you, huh?" he said. "Probably shat right in your pants, didn't you?"

He looked at me, then slapped his leg and cackled.

"Kind of wish I could have seen that. You just a-walking along minding your own and then ba-BOOM! flat on your ass. Damn, I sure wish I could have seen it." Once he quit laughing, he stomped off toward the house and hollered over his shoulder, "Leave it. Be some hot spots for a few days. Just leave it be for now."

I never told him it was me, though I almost did. Let him believe what he thinks happened and damn it all to hell. If I hadn't burned it, it was likely to have happened the exact way he described it—some other time and somebody or somebodies else standing where I was or closer—and that would have been real trouble. Law couldn't have looked away from a couple of crispy bodies no matter how much they were in for with Lester. I say "almost did," because one night, a few nights after the coop, Lester and me were sitting at the table in the kitchen eating our dinner of beans—one can each—and Dinty Moore—split two ways between us. All of a sudden, Lester said, "A man's got to choose for himself and if what he chooses bothers some other people, well, they can choose to go a different route. But a man can do as he pleases."

I thought about the coop and how much that pleased me. But Lester continued.

"You're only free as you let yourself be," he said and that made me feel good, feel squared up. So I just about said what I did with the coop, but Lester kept going—

"Thinking about your daddy," he said. "Thinking that if he is in jail or if he ain't or even if he do have another family out there, let him be happy. Why the hell not?"

I half nodded and shuffled my beans around on my plate and kept my mouth shut.

Here's why I like fire: It's alive. About the only thing really alive I can think of. Aliver than you and me. The way it does exactly what it wants to do, the way it takes what it wants, the way it leaves its mark—in scorched timbers and blackened roof beams, exploded gas tanks and blown-out glass. Hell, I once saw a completely burned car where the fire was so intense the chassis had liquefied and run down the sewer. The way it can climb a building in grand glorious style or the way it can sit and smolder, then pounce whenever it wants. Utterly silent sometimes. I like those cat qualities. Fire is a mountain lion. But noisy as hell other times, a stomping machine marauding through the western wilderness, scattering elk and mule deer. It's the glowing rash on a mountainside. Some symptom of some unpronounceable sex disease straight from hell. I like to talk about fire. To imagine fire. To do fire.

In the end, they finally busted Uncle Lester, as you might have guessed. He's in for a long stretch in federal lock-up, last I heard down in Yazoo City, which means me and him will likely never cross paths again. The county had held elections, elections he didn't bother to vote in, and the good people of the county chose a brand new head lawman—"Victor Creswell for Sheriff! Tough on crime!" I remember the local cable ad went—and Sheriff Creswell made good on his word. About fifty squad cars eased their way up the rocky drive, no lights, no sirens. When I saw them coming, I jumped underneath a low-branched pine tree at the edge of the woods near Lester's barn lab, hunkered down, and watched. They surrounded it. One of them got on the bullhorn and shouted for Lester to come out. And like he just hadn't heard right, Lester poked his head out of the huge barn door. As if to say "Come again?" Those deputies threw him down and trampled all over him so that by the time they got him into a squad car, they must have broke every rib in his chest. I heard him shouting, real words at first—"I got rights! I got rights!"—then screaming cusses, then chuffing sobs. Him banging on that backseat window was the last I ever saw of him. A skinny deputy with glasses and a windbreaker took a bunch of pictures of the barn with a huge camera, then went inside where I presume he took a bunch more.

They'd all left Lester's barn by evening and it stood there alone, stark and naked, but I waited until it got completely dark before rolling out from under the pine tree. They'd be back in the morning. A weird mist lit by starlight was hovering over the fields. I ghosted through it to the big barn door and put my hands on the rough wood— thick planks towering up to the eaves where the owls roosted. It took some shoving, more than I expected, to roll the door back a few feet. I slipped inside. If darker than dark was a shade of dark, this was it. The kind of endless black you might find inside a coffin. Oh lonesome me here in the darkest place in the world. I sure about panicked.

I'd taken to toting igniters in my pockets at all times. Call them security measures if you want to. Like the way a little kid drags along his worn-out teddy bear everyplace he goes—one hand in his father's, one hand clutching the bear tight to his chest. For me, it was usually four or five books of matches, sometimes ten and usually a couple of lighters and it gave me peace. I can't explain why. Just that it did. I could think clearer. I could act clearer. So, I got out a couple of my matchbooks and one of my lighters and lit the matchbooks and tossed them around inside the barn, listening to them pop and fizz when the little flame touched all the matches. I threw one to my left and one to my right and one straight ahead and damn it all if the one straight ahead didn't land on something flammable. A big blue flame jumped up, like I'd summoned a demon to that place. It rose straight from the barn floor and danced its way higher, consuming what looked to me like black organ pipes. I watched it change from blue to orange to bright white and those pipes melted and as the light from the fire rolled through the barn, I could see other things I'd never seen before, other shapes that looked mean: big red drums and short black drums, tall-necked glass things, and squat, wide glass things. Shadows splashing over everything, receding, splashing again.

I hightailed it out of there back to the woods, found my pine tree and scrabbled up, branches and needles I couldn't see raking my face, whapping at my head and arms and legs. I guess I got to about twenty or thirty feet when the roof of the barn sort of burst—a piece of it actually caved in, but it sent up such a sudden eruption of flame and spark it looked like somebody'd bombed it. In no time at all the barn was overwhelmed and the fire was too hot, so I had to squirrel down and when I heard sirens in the distance I fled into the dark.

I must not have gotten all that far, because when I woke up where I'd lain down—finally had to quit running on account of just not being able to see anything—I could still smell the smoke, the acid tinge in the cool morning mist. Kept walking then—walking and walking through the woods, and twisting my ankles in leaf-covered snake holes—finally arriving at an empty old farmhouse. Nobody'd been in it for years. So, what the hell, I moved in. Set up shop on the second floor in one of the bedrooms. Shat in their outhouse. Washed up and drank from the creek in the ravine nearby. And I was happy. I pinched what I needed Sunday mornings from neighbors' houses. Hell, nearest "neighbors" were miles away, so I got my exercise. I only pinched what I needed to live on. I don't steal. Bread, canned soup, Oreos or popsicles if I was feeling luxurious. Sunday mornings because they all went to church and I figured hell if they were so good and holy they'd not mind giving a little to a poor hungry stranger. That was me! I never actually took more than what I needed to survive. And survive I did. I don't know how long I lived there, but it must have been months. Until the leaves on the trees started to redden.

One chilly night I came home—treated myself to a movie ten miles away—and there was a little round light bouncing in the living room. The end of a beam of a flashlight. Next to the house was a vehicle I didn't recognize. I stood and stared and couldn't believe it. Just flabbergasted all to hell. The beam was in the living room. I could see it through the big picture window up front. After I got my wits back, I crept around to the back of the house. Took my boots off and carried them in my hand so the floor wouldn't squeak. Tiptoed through the kitchen and now I was hearing their voices, low voices, whispers between a boy and a girl, strange voices, the voices of aliens. The boy voice said, "Here? Or here?" and she was saying, "Right here. No... no... here." I froze and waited, and then heard shuffling, and then came the sounds of saliva on skin and their tongues smacking and sliding over one another like salamanders wriggling in the muck.

I don't want you to get the wrong impression about me. I got nothing against love. I know I ain't never had it. But I hope to have it someday—meet the right girl, pop out a couple kids. That does sound just right. Of course I got some work to do first, self-work they call it, and who doesn't have self-work to do? You do, I do, we all do. But if you get a little better every day, well, you ain't never going to get to perfect, so forget that, but you'll eventually grow up, at least a little. Choose right, do good, be a man, be free. I say that to myself every single day now.

18 THE WORST FLOPHOUSE IN HEAVEN

The hotel's elevator was broken. Gene had to climb the stairs to the third floor and then walk back down. When he got back to the front desk, he opened the key box, threw a set of keys in, and then plunked into the chair behind the desk. His chest and gut were heaving. He shoved his hand into the pocket of his jeans, pulled out his albuterol inhaler and sucked on it once, twice, a third time. Then he leaned back. After he caught his breath, he ran his fingers through his hair and sighed.

Ray came in the front door of the hotel and stomped the snow off his boots. He was breathing hard, too, but he wasn't fat like Gene. He was skinny and hunched and wiry hair stuck out from under his stocking cap. The thick lenses of his glasses were fogged. He was smoking a cigarette and the smoke made a pale wreath around his head.

"Go on upstairs," Gene said.

"I just come in," Ray said.

"You're drunk. Go on up to your room. Go to bed."

"I just come in."

"You didn't get no mail," Gene said, "if you're wondering."

"None?"

"No mail, no messages. Nobody wants to talk to you. Now go to bed."

"What makes you think I'm drunk?" Ray said.

"Because you're a goddamn drunk, you're all the time drunk." Gene's words came out of his mouth like they always did, like they were being shoved out.

The front desk was as old as the hotel, probably nearly eighty years old, and the top drawer stuck. Gene banged it side to side and popped it open. He shoved his fat hand in and fished around for the remote. When he found it, he flipped on the TV hanging on the wall across from the front desk. The ten o'clock news appeared, half-over.

Ray tottered across the lobby to the grungy coffee pot sitting on the warmer next to the microwave. He poured the last of it into a Styrofoam cup, his hand jiggling. The coffee sloshed down the side of the cup as he poured.

"Damn, that's hot," he said.

Steam swirled out of the cup, melding with the smoke from his cigarette. He came back to the front desk and leaned on it, looking at the TV. He slurped at the coffee and said, "This tastes like shit."

"Cause it's been sitting there about four, five hours. Burnt to hell probably," Gene said.

"Well, it shastes like tit. Tastes like shit, I mean." Ray laughed his head off.

Gene rolled his eyes. He stood, yanked his jeans up, and crashed back into his chair. The springs moaning under his weight covered Ray's cackle.

They looked at the TV for a while until Ray said, "Damn near busted my ass on the ice. Fell right on my ass getting off the bus, right up here at North and California."

Gene didn't say anything.

"Hey," Ray said, "I said I fell on my ass."

"Oh yeah? I would have laughed my ass off had I seen that," Gene said.

"I bet you would have. Thanks a lot."

"Sure, Ray."

"Yeah, thanks a lot, old buddy old pal. Thanks a whole lot."

Gene's eyes flitted around the lobby of the hotel. Nobody was in the lobby but he and Ray. Out the front door, it was snowing. Gene folded his hands across his gut. Then he unfolded them, ran his fingers through his greasy hair again, and stacked and then unstacked the small boxes of paperclips on the desk. Ray leaned and smoked. When he finished the cigarette he threw it on the floor and crushed it out with his boot heel. Then he lit a new one. He held the pack out to Gene, a fresh one poking up, but Gene didn't see it right away. When he did, he said, "I got asthma—you know that—why you want to give me a cigarette?"

"Suit yourself." The end of Ray's cigarette glowed and then dirty smoke rolled out of his nose in Gene's direction.

The news cut to a commercial for Luna flooring and the jingle pinged around the lobby.

Gene said, "Ray, you know Tommy across the hall from you in 313?"

"Junky Tommy? The skinny kid?" Ray said.

"Yeah, Junky Tommy. Anybody ever come see him?"

"You'd know better than me, your ass behind this desk all day long."

"I'm just here my shift, asshole. Nobody I know ever come see him. You never saw nobody come up see him?"

"I don't pay attention that much. I don't know, a girl or two sometimes. But it's not like he has a girlfriend or something. Hookers, probably."

"How can he afford hookers?"

"I don't know, maybe not. Maybe they're just girls he shoots up with."

"Junkies, too, probably."

"Junky hookers. They're pretty cheap, I bet. Skanky, though. Gotta clean them up first. Give them a bath, you know," Ray said and laughed again.

"Must be hard to be a junky," Gene said.

"Why do you ask?" Ray said.

"I was just wondering."

"Why do you care, though?"

"I don't care. I don't give a shit one way or the other."

"Nobody comes to see him."

"He goes out a lot, though. Out and back, out and back."

"He's going out to score all the time, that's why."

"I know that. He hasn't been down tonight, though."

"No?"

"Nope."

"Maybe he's shacking up with one of his dirty junky hookers tonight."

"No, he's here."

"What, he owes you money or something?"

"No, he don't owe me money. I was just thinking about him."

"Don't tell me you owe him money."

"Nobody owes nobody no money, Ray."

"Then why the hell are you thinking about Junky Tommy?"

"I was just asking. I don't care about the guy." Gene pitched his weight forward and back a couple of times and the chair springs underneath him screeched. He shuffled through a stack of letters for the long-term hotel residents who hadn't paid their rent the last month.

"Why don't you go to bed, okay? I got work to do," Gene said.

"Sure, Gene. Looks like you got your hands full flipping through those papers there. Geez," Ray said.

Gene didn't say anything. On the news the anchor cut

to a story about a woman in Niles who was murdered by her husband. He'd stabbed her with a K-BAR knife and shoved her body into their junior high son's hockey bag before dumping it in a reservoir. Some lady found her half-frozen in the ice while she was walking her dog.

"You ever see a dead body before?" Gene said.

"My mother's funeral," Ray said.

"Besides that. I mean a real dead body," Gene said.

"My mother doesn't count as a real dead body? I saw her. She was dead. Or else they put the wrong lady in the casket," Ray laughed.

"Not all dolled up at a wake," Gene said.

Ray kept talking about his mother. "If that woman walked into this hotel alive right now, you'd see me take a giant shit right here on the floor. Ma, ma, you're alive! Why, God? Why, God? Uh, I mean, thank God! Thank God!"

"It's not like in the movies," Gene said.

"I'd kill her myself if she walked in here. I'd make damn sure she was dead."

"Don't say things like that." Gene's voice was quiet. He looked at Ray and Ray looked back up at the news. He didn't say anything else about his mother.

"In the movies, the body just lays there, eyes closed. Looks asleep, but they're supposed to be dead. That ain't dead. That ain't how it looks," Gene said.

"How do you know?"

Gene coughed and then said, "When I was a kid down by Springfield my uncle took me hunting. Found a dead hunter. Shot through the head with his own gun. Accident or suicide we couldn't tell. Looked frightful, just frightful."

"How long had he been dead?"

"A long time, probably. Maybe even a year. No eyes in the eye sockets, side of his skull busted through. Looked like a coyote'd been gnawing on his leg bone, too."

"Nobody missed him, apparently."

"That's what I remember thinking most. Why's he still out here under this tree instead of in the ground somewhere? What, don't nobody know him? Somebody forget about him?"

"How old were you?"

"I don't know, eleven, twelve."

"You sure had something to tell about at show and tell."

"I didn't say nothing about it for a long time. To nobody."

"Well, that would fuck me up," Ray said. He tipped the coffee cup back and swallowed the last of it like he was drinking water. His Adam's apple bobbed a couple of times. Then he said, "Okay, Gene, I'm going up to my room. A very, very pleasant good evening to you."

"My uncle never said anything about it either, not to me or my aunt or anybody else. When we first saw what it was, I mean when we first realized it was a dead body against that tree, he said, 'Look away, Gene, look away,' but I looked—I couldn't help it—and he seen I looked so he grabbed me and shoved me back the direction we come from. I couldn't think about no deer that day. We even seen some, but I couldn't shoot. Neither could he," Ray said.

"You should've put one of your tags on the dead guy and hauled him back with you. Tied him to the fender. Stuffed him and mounted him in the living room." Ray's laugh turned into a hack of a cough.

"Fuck you, go on up to your room." Gene's eyebrows squeezed together and the corners of his mouth drew down a little.

"Kidding, I'm kidding," Ray said, after he stopped choking. "Fine. See you later. Good fucking night to you, Gene."

Ray turned and jabbed the elevator button once and when nothing happened he jabbed it again and then again. Gene watched him.

"What's wrong with the elevator?"

"Busted."

"Since when?"

"Since earlier."

"Don't put a damn sign on it or anything."

"Third floor's not far, just walk."

Ray grabbed the handle of the door that went to the stairs, but his fingers slipped off and he stumbled backwards. He muttered and cursed, then yanked the door open and stepped into the stairwell. The door slammed shut behind him and Gene was alone in the lobby. He flipped the TV off.

For a long time, Gene sat at the desk staring at the wall. The stucco was cracked and the valleys and crannies of the stucco were highlighted with black dust and second-hand smoke that had built up over the years. The radiators clicked and hissed. Yellow light radiated through the lobby, filtered by the thick shades on the lamps by the couch. Outside, the snow was falling harder and it occurred to Gene that he should put on his parka, shovel a layer off the sidewalk in front of the hotel and throw salt down, but he couldn't bring himself to do it. He thought it would be alright anyway. Not too many people were out because the weather was supposed to get worse, nobody else was coming for a room tonight and the long-termers were mostly inside already. Besides the junky long-termers. There were only two or three besides Junky Tommy, and like Junky Tommy, they came and went all night long. Gene thought if a junky slipped on the ice he probably wouldn't feel it doped up on junk. Then he thought about Ray slipping and falling on the ice by the bus stop and a bolt of a desire to laugh shot through him, but he didn't, couldn't.

He turned to the locker that held the spare room keys, a green box that was starting to rust, fixed to the wall next to the grid of mail slots. The door swung open on its loose hinges. The keys, notched metal flakes, some gold, some silver, stacked in uneven piles at the bottom of the locker, almost fell out onto the floor, as they almost did every time he opened the locker door. Each key was tagged with a blue disc that had a room number stamped on it. Gene shuffled through the pile, the pile jangling as he pushed through it, and found the key with the 313 blue disc tag on top in the back. This went into the pocket that also held his albuterol. Gene checked the lobby over his shoulder, slid from behind the front desk and walked to the stairwell. He pulled the stairwell door open, the handle cold to his pudgy hands.

When he got to the third floor he was wheezing through his nose and gaping mouth. He sounded to himself like a pig in heat. He stood at the third-floor stairwell entrance, then doubled over, hands on his knees. He fumbled for his albuterol and sucked out the medicine. He waited until his breathing was under control and then walked down the hall. He tried to hold his breath and his heavy footsteps were hushed by the thick, cheap carpeting.

Outside 313, Gene stopped and cocked his head. He heard the low hum of Ray's TV coming through the door across the hall. There was dull light seeping under the door too. Gene imagined Ray sprawled out on his bed, half-downed tub of vodka in his hand, looking at an infomercial for miracle detergent, or a judge show, or an episode of CSI, a rerun with David Caruso standing over a bloody body in a sterile lab. Gene thought this is how Ray would drift off to sleep. It's how he imagined Ray drifted off to sleep every night—a black, empty sleep without dreams, without even a twitch of his body until the light of the next day jammed itself under his eyelids.

Gene slid the key into the lock of 313. It made a jagged sound, metal scraping metal. Gene turned it and the lock ka-chunked. He pushed on the door and it swung open. He caught the smell of the room in the back of his throat. It was old grease from the frying pan on the hot-plate and decaying sweat wafting up from the piles of clothes on the floor. It was mouse shit and mouse piss in the corners where the wall met the floor, where the tiny bastards had marked their trails in and out of the room. It was confined air, dank and heavy. And there was the smell of flesh in the air, exposed flesh, flesh that had stopped being cared for. Flesh that had just begun to break down, to tear itself apart with its own juices. It was the acrid sting of death rising from Junky Tommy's body somewhere in the dark. It was not yet overpowering, but it was gradually taking over the host of other smells that mixed together in Junky Tommy's room.

Gene turned on the light. The bulbs in the ceiling fixture were all burned out except one, and whatever wattage it was, it was low. It barely swept the shadows from the center of the room. Light drifted in from the fixture on the crooked pole in the alley outside Tommy's window, but this light somehow seemed to make no difference in the room. Tommy's body was lying on the floor next to his bed. He didn't have a shirt on and there were purple splotches on his caved-in chest, welts that surfed the skin stretched over his ribs. Gene could see that some of the larger welts were now starting to ooze a thin, clear liquid. Tommy's arms were bent at the elbows, and his hands were frozen in half-fists, like he was about to grab something he didn't think he would be able to hold onto. Up and down his forearms were needle tracks so heavy it looked like they'd been tattooed on. The muscles in Tommy's neck were stuck tensed, creating lines from his skinny shoulders running up and underneath his jaw, which jutted forward. The same liquid was starting to ooze from between his drawn lips and his small, pointed nose. Residue of a dried, white froth spilled from his mouth down his cheek and disappeared into a dark spot in the carpet. Tommy's eyes were pale, the brown circles in the middle had faded, too, and they looked like they had ice covering them, the way a puddle in the park looks when it dips below freezing. Tommy was looking up, like he was trying to see something in his hair, but from how his body was lying on its side, his eyes were actually pointed at his rig sitting on the floor. The needle was empty and the spoon burned black.

Gene moved toward the body. He shook his head and his eyebrows lifted and scrunched together. He covered his mouth, and stood staring at Tommy. After a few minutes, his arms went out to his sides, like he was about to flap them and take off, but he balanced himself and then lowered himself to his knees, his gut pulling him down faster than he was ready for, and he nearly fell forward onto Tommy's body. He braced himself on the floor and straightened. Then he reached toward Tommy, his fat index finger touching the skin of his cheek. The skin was cold and rough, like a motorcycle jacket. It didn't feel like human skin. Gene yanked his hand away, but then reached out again, this time allowing his entire hand to cup Tommy's cheek. Gene's lips formed Tommy's name, but no sound came out.

In an instant, Gene pictured Tommy's last living moment in a hundred possible ways. The body, emptied of life before it even hit the carpet, smashing onto its side as the real Tommy abandoned it forever. Or, Tommy falling like a tree chopped down by a lightning strike, shocked to death, alone and filling with rage on the other side, wherever that was, because the fat front desk man was the first to see his half-naked corpse. Or the worst, Tommy twitching and flopping about by the bed, seizing, convulsing, reaching out with the last rays of his perception to others somewhere, people only he could see, people only he knew, people who could not hear him or see him or possibly even know that in another instant he would be gone and the skin and bones and tissue of his leftover body would begin to devour themselves.

Gene gulped in a breath, pulled the collar of his shirt up over his mouth and nose and pushed both arms under Tommy's body. It was freezing and the skin on Tommy's back was so thin that Gene was afraid he would rip it. The

146

other arm cradled Tommy's knees. Then he stood. Cracking sounds came from Tommy's joints and his head flopped back, his neck cracking the loudest, and his matted hair waved. Gene was surprised at how easy it was to lift and move him. He put him on the bed. He was breathing hard again. The liquid seeping from Tommy's body stuck to Gene's arms, so that when he stepped back, little transparent lines of it bowed downward before breaking off. Gene wiped them on the sides of his shirt, which was spotted on the front with the fluid, too.

Tommy's body on the bed retained the shape it had when Gene picked him up—knees bent, back arched, head thrown back and jaw open, like a great scream was about to escape. Gene stared at the body, and then lifted Tommy's head and slid a pillow underneath. He forced the lids closed over the eyes and he tried to shut Tommy's mouth, but it wouldn't stay shut. So after a couple attempts, Gene gave up.

Gene shuffled to the end of the bed and grabbed Tommy's ankles. Tommy was still wearing a pair of canvas high-tops, and the feeling of the canvas in Gene's grip seemed strange and foreign. He tugged on Tommy's legs, but they did not straighten out. Gene shuffled to the side of the bed again and reached over the body, grabbing Tommy's right ankle and pulling it while at the same time pressing down hard on Tommy's right knee with his other hand. There was another pronounced pop and then a stiff crunch and the leg straightened out. Then he did the same to Tommy's left leg. Next, he forced Tommy's arms towards each other, across his sunken torso. When the hands finally touched, Gene pressed the palms together and laced Tommy's fingers, braiding them into a position of penitence and prayer at his waist. Then Gene stepped back. Now the light from the streetlight outside was noticeable. It came through the window and alighted on the length of Tommy's body, perching on it like a delicate layer of dust. Tommy looked like a ghoul begging God to let him live even in the broom closet of the worst flophouse in heaven.

It didn't look right. It looked awful. Gene glanced around the room and saw, in the corner in one of the piles of laundry, what looked like a wadded up bedsheet. He grabbed it and started pulling it out, but then an army of roaches burst from it and scurried in every direction. Gene dropped it. He looked back at Tommy, whose head had rolled on the pillow a little, so it was facing to the right. It looked like Tommy was trying to see out the window into the alley. Gene straightened the head and arranged the pillow around it so it wouldn't move.

Then he went to Tommy's closet. Inside, there were a few hangers and hanging from them were two black t-shirts and a light blue one, and a pair of jeans on a hook. On the floor were two old speakers for a stereo system that was nowhere in the room. There was barely anything else anywhere. Gene sighed, then stooped and picked up the sheet again. He held it at arm's length and shook it out. It had holes in it and stains. He brought it to the bed and draped it over Tommy's body. Then he tucked it under the body, starting at Tommy's shoulders, down one side, around the legs, and up the other side. Gene left Tommy's head uncovered and tried one more time to close his mouth, but it wouldn't stay closed. Now it looked like Tommy was trying to sing, like he was a starving angel wrapped up in white, performing a number for his share of the heavenly feast. That didn't look quite right either. Gene untucked the sheet and pulled it off Tommy's body. He wadded it up again and threw it in the corner. Gene put his hands on his hips and looked at Tommy's contorted corpse.

Just then, from behind him, Gene heard his name. It whipped into the room like a hatchet thrown at his back. Gene gasped and flung his body around. He hadn't closed the door behind him when he came into Tommy's room and there was Ray, glasses sliding down his nose, eyes fisheyed behind them. His hooded sweatshirt seemed to hang halfway down his legs and his legs stuck out below like two stalks propping him up.

"Hey, Gene?" Ray said.

"He's dead," Gene said.

"Tommy's dead?"

"Yeah."

Gene stared at Ray and Ray hung his head. He put his hand out and leaned on the door frame. Neither of them said anything and Gene didn't know how long Ray had been standing behind him watching.

"Aw, geez," Ray said, after a few seconds. His voice cracked. Then he sniffed a little and ran the sleeve of his sweatshirt across his mustache.

"It's pretty bad," Gene said.

"Holy shit, that's disgusting." Ray's head kicked backward a little as he sniffed the air. He stopped leaning on the doorframe and stood up straight.

"He died earlier. His neighbor, the little old Chinese man next door, Mr. What's-His-Name, called me up here because he heard these sounds coming from in here and then a falling sound, he said, and then crying." The words blubbered out of Gene's mouth.

"Did you call the cops?"

"I was going to. Earlier when I first found out but I went back down and then you and I started talking so after you came back up I came back up," Gene said and then he added, "to make sure."

"Wait, you knew Tommy was dead the whole time we were downstairs talking?" Ray said.

"Yeah."

"When I came in tonight?"

"Yeah."

Ray inched into the room. Gene didn't move. He tried to make his body seem even bigger. Ray stopped a few feet in front of Gene and craned his neck, peaking around Gene's girth. Ray's eyes widened.

"You're sick," Ray said.

"I'm not sick, Ray, he just didn't look ready to go."

"Well, what the fuck were you going to do, Gene, embalm him?"

"Make him presentable."

"Presentable to who? The cops? They just zip him up and throw him in the wagon. They don't give a shit what he looks like," Ray said.

"I'm saying somebody would give a shit."

"Who?"

"I don't know."

"His mother? His father? His skinny heroin whores?"

"Me, if nobody else. Me then."

"You."

"Yeah."

Ray put his hands on his hips. He teetered back and forth. His lips were wet. From behind him, light from the hallway was curling into Junky Tommy's room.

"Gene, I'm calling the cops right now to come get that festering fucking body out of here." Ray's voice was quivering.

"Hold on, Ray."

"I'm not fucking holding on." He turned and swayed out of the room.

Gene turned back to Tommy's body. He walked toward it and smoothed the hair across Tommy's forehead. He gazed at the body and was quiet.

19 THE END OF FUN

Andy kicked the wide, glass front doors of Phoenix First National Bank out of his way and stuffed the .38 into the back of his jeans. He leaped down the marble steps, skidding in his cowboy boots, all the while trailed by rogue bills—hundreds and fifties contorting little escapes from his pockets and the bulging pillowcase in his left hand. He hollered, "Yeehaw!" and fumbled with some keys, hollered, "Fuck you!" over his shoulder, yanked open the driver's door of the rusty blue Camry, jumped in, and was gone. A pale cloud of toasted rubber, asphalt, and a few lazy bills spun in the desert breeze.

He didn't stop till Wickenburg, almost into Yavapai County. The Camry was about out of gas anyway, so he filled it up, stole some Red Bull, and then pulled into the McDonald's parking lot. Robbing banks will leave a body famished. Just a completely hollow gut. Andy felt it bad, a bulb of an ache right below his stick-out ribs. He sat in the car for a few minutes, patted his skinny belly, then smoked a cigarillo down to the plastic tip. Checking over his shoulder, too. There was nobody. He got out.

"Couple of quarter-pounders, give me two fries, too, big sized, and the biggest Coke you got."

"Will that be all?"

"Throw a couple of pies in there, too. Make 'em apple."

The kid pushed a few buttons, red ones and blue ones, and then the total popped up. He handed the kid some money.

"Oh," the kid said.

"You ever seen one of them before? Probably not."

"I can't give you change, not from this drawer. I'll check with my manager."

Andy's hand shot out and grabbed the kid's scrawny wrist. "Don't check with your manger. I don't need no change. Hell, keep it yourself. I'm starving, so hurry on up."

The kid's eyes bulged. Big brown circles in big white ones. He looked like he was about to say something, but then he straightened and worked his arm loose of Andy's grip.

"Keep it?"

"Keep it all."

The kid put the bill in the drawer, under the till.

Andy was the only customer in the place. He chomped and slurped and stared out at the desert. It went on forever. There were cacti and low, jagged mountains off in the distance, all of it baked by the sun, baked by it for, what, thousands of years, millions maybe. Baked down to little nubs of plants and rocks, with little stunted animals creeping and darting here and there. Everything cooked off but the main guts of some ancient, spooky geology. Water sometimes choked out of the hard sand here and there, enough to make dark brown circles that took about five minutes to evaporate completely. That's what they call springs. Nothing but a tease. Andy pulled out his cell phone, touched some buttons, put it to his ear. The call went right to voicemail.

"Mama," he said, cupping the phone to his mouth, "it's Andy. I been thinking about home. Sis told me you buried Tommy in April. Can't say I'll miss the sumnabitch. I know you're gonna, for some damn reason. You got your reasons, Mama, I know you got 'em."

Andy's eyes swooped around the McDonald's.

"I just love my mama. I just love her. Andy loves his mama." He flipped the phone shut and wiped his eyes with the tough skin on the back of his hand, and then stuck the phone back in his pocket. He stuffed the quarter-pounder wrappers into the fry boxes, drank off his Coke, and picked up the pies. He went back to the register. In two seconds, the barrel of the .38 was between the kid's eyes.

"Changed my mind. Let me get that bill back, plus whatever else's in there."

The kid was frozen.

"Did I just make you piss yourself?"

"No."

"I'm nice enough. Don't I look nice? Look at my face. It's a nice face, ain't it?"

"I guess so?"

"You guess so? Let me ask you something, and be honest. You like your job?"

"What?"

"I like my job. I like my job real well."

"Hey." The manager, who this probably was, a bald middle-aged man with a clean white shirt and a black bow-tie with teensy Golden Arches all over it.

"Hi there. I'm sticking up your employee here."

"Don't hurt anybody." The manager held his hands up, palms out.

"Hurry up, son," Andy said, eyes on the manager.

"Give it to him, James," the manager said.

"James. Why don't you shove it in that bag there?"

James stuffed the drawer's green contents into a to-go bag.

"You want the change, too?" James said.

"Look at this customer service," Andy said. "No, I don't. Thank you for asking. And give James here a raise, would you?"

The manager nodded, but didn't make eye contact with either of them.

"Hey, do me one favor before I go, James."

The kid's face was blank.

"Why don't you get a cheeseburg. Go on. Then bring it out here."

When the kid got back, with the small loafey thing wrapped in yellow, Andy said, "Now, heave it up into the air. Wait. Ain't enough room in here. Come on, we're going outside. You, too, let's go. Get all your people from the back. Get 'em. Make it quick."

Andy directed the manager around the restaurant with the gun barrel. The manager spoke in a strained voice, panic leaking into his words. He was whispering mainly, but it was like his brain wanted to scream. Everybody filed outside into the parking lot, a platoon of maroon-shirted, black-hatted kids, then the manager in white, then Andy.

"You got that cheeseburg, James? Watch this. Heave it up as high as you can."

The kid looked at Andy with pinched-together eyebrows.

"Well, come on."

The kid reared back and threw the cheeseburger so high and hard he left his feet. Andy aimed and fired—a miss. The crack echoed off the McDonald's windows and rolled away out into the desert. The cheeseburger plopped down on the pavement. Nobody said a word. Andy stepped to the burger and fired a shot into it, meat and pickles and shredded bun flying all over his boots.

"That got it." He looked up. "See you all."

Fifteen minutes out into the desert, there appeared suddenly a band of mustangs along an old barbed-wire-topped fence that vanished with the I-10 over the horizon. Andy whooped and stomped on the breaks, and the little Camry fishtailing to a halt on the shoulder. He leaped out, slammed the door, and then scrambled up the berm to the fence, little cascades of brittle granite sliding away under his boots. He watched the horses run. He howled, his voice ragged and sputtering on the lingering dust cloud. Several hundred yards away, the horses wheeled, scrabbling over each other, and romped back. Andy's breath caught in his throat. He got as close to the fence as he could, close enough almost to get his chin hung up on the barbed wire.

The animals were magnificent. The thunder of their hooves rattled his teeth. Out shot their forelegs and back under their massive bodies they curled over and over, huge, angular chunks of the hard-packed sand flying up against the sky. Most all had white blazes from blonde forelocks on down to their pink and gray speckled noses, the nostrils flared and pulsing with each voracious intake of breath. Their manes and tails flamed out behind them. And the sweat darkened their massive flanks, patches of wet down their bare hides, giving shape and definition to the rolling muscle. When they were past, a spray of wind and stink and grit slapped Andy on the back and he stared after them with his mouth hanging open.

The horses wheeled again. They charged back along the fence, unaware of anything else, it seemed, except each other and the ability to run. They nicked, bit, whinnied, shoved. Once again they were almost upon him, only a few feet on the other side of the fence. Andy smiled, closed his eyes, and threw his head back, drinking the same heated air into his lungs the horses were drinking into theirs. He laughed, a long, rolling laugh that poured out of him like a monsoon waterfall blasting between rocks.

And then a snap, then a scream. The horses suddenly cleared off, each running in its direction, except one. A stallion, screaming so hard its tongue shot straight from its mouth, a pink slab wedged between yellow-white teeth, gray lips curled back. White flecks of froth in the corners of the horse's mouth. With each scream, its entire body shook. It reared up on its hind legs over and over, bucking and snorting, and its eyes were on fire. Andy, ducking the barbed wire, pressed into the fence.

The animal's right front leg had snapped at the fetlock, its hoof now swinging freely. It moved like a sock with a bar of soap in the toe. The animal's rear legs gave out and it stumbled and fell, its entire weight crashing down on the wounded leg and the horse screamed louder, bitter screams that ripped the air. But the animal clamored up, tossing its head and leaping, raising a thin brown cloud in the air around itself. The fall had compounded the fracture, and Andy could see the stark white of pointed bone sticking through the skin, the chestnut of the coat around the fetlock reddening.

"Ohnoshit," Andy whispered.

The horse danced in a circle, almost breaking its neck, its broad back rolling and snapping as if it was trying to throw an invisible rider. Just for a second, Andy's eyes came square with one of the horse's, a glazed-over orb. The thing was trying to say something. The head bobbed again, the eyes now heavenward, and it would not stop screaming.

Andy scrambled back to the Camry, slipping on the loose gravel. He ripped into the car by the passenger door, grabbed the .38 from the seat, cussed again, and fairly flew back up to the fence. The wounded horse had bounded away, about fifty yards off.

"Horse, I can't shoot that far," Andy yelled. "Horse!"

The horse was in the gun's sights now, the gun quivering in Andy's hands. He tried to hold the weapon the way he'd seen police do it. It was hard to aim at the bouncing thing. "Horse," he called again. Then he fired.

The stallion leaped sideways. Squinting, Andy could see a little button of red on the horse's flank and the animal stumbled. It flipped its head like it was trying to look behind itself. He fired again and the horse fell over, but its legs beat the air, the injured one below the broken fetlock spinning like a pinwheel at the top of the leg.

Andy slithered under the fence, tearing a sleeve on a hidden nail in the fencepost. He bolted to the horse and found it sputtering blood, crimson running in little washes down the chestnut hide. When it saw him, it made a lame attempt to get its legs under itself, but could not and tipped back onto the ground. Long, drooping lines of blood like cables from the corners of its mouth tethered the beast to the sand.

Andy caught himself staring. Who knows how long. Before him, the horse rolled, cried, flipped its massive body around in the sand, but every time it made a move, the next one would be less, and the one after that less. Andy rubbed his eyes. Two more steps and the horse's head was square at his feet, still now except for a tremor every few seconds. He held the gun at the angle of the eye and the ear. The horse looked at him and he fired. The head bounced against the sand, the tongue, slimed with black blood, lolled from the mouth and pretty soon a wash of deep red blood flowed out, collecting dust and tiny pebbles and dried petals of yellow and light from the desert floor and pushing on, outward like an expanding halo.

Andy sat down. Little breaths puttered between his lips and the sweat dripped down his forehead, stinging his eyes, speckling his blue jeans as it dripped from his nose, cheeks, and chin. He wiped his forehead with the back of his hand, the hand still clutching the black rubber grip of the .38. The gun was heavy. He set it down at his feet. He sat by the horse a long time, thinking about vultures and when they'd show and would they think him a dead thing also, would they pick and peck at his skin, would they strip his bones.

When he stood, the sky was changing. The sun had sunk below the western rim of the world, leaving a glowing orange crust, a line of smoldering embers sprinkled across the tops of the scraggy mountains far away. A blanket of black was falling on the horizon from the east with snags of starlight and two or three burning rips of meteors. He stooped and picked up the gun. There was one shell left. Two at the burger, three in the horse, so one left in the cylinder. He stuffed it in his belt at the back of his jeans and ambled heavy-footed back to the fence. He turned. There was the carcass. The dark mound looked like a rock outcropping. A piece of the desert. An old piece of the desert changed into a new piece anyway. He sunk down, slid under the fence and walked-slid across the berm to the car. It took a couple of tries, but the engine crashed to life, the headlights came on, and Andy drove off down the I-10 into the night.

At the diner, Neon Slim's, somebody recognized him. A barrel-chested rancher type with a dyed black mustache and rusty boot spurs. He stepped over to Andy's booth in the corner and stood beside it. Andy looked up.

"So," the rancher type said, "you hear the one about the horse and the bar? This horse walks into a bar and the bartender says, 'Why the long face?'"

"That was funny when I first heard it about a hundred years ago." Andy didn't look at the man.

"Well," the man said, "I seen you got a long face. Chin up, son."

Andy stared at the napkin dispenser.

"I know you," the rancher type said.

"I don't think so."

"I think so. Mind if I sit?" And he sat across the table from Andy without waiting for a 'yes' or a 'no.' The man smiled and folded his hands on the tabletop. They were chubby hands with red fingers, the left ring finger sporting a dinged-up wedding band. The thin skin around his eyes wrinkled when he smiled. He looked like a grandpa. Maybe he wanted to sell oatmeal. Andy put the coffee cup down on the table. He'd just swigged off the dregs.

"I didn't say for you to sit."

"I know it."

Andy glared. The man gazed.

"My name's Clark, Ted Clark." The man didn't offer his hand for a shake.

"Okay."

"And you are?"

"Han Solo."

Clark chuckled, signaled to the waitress and when she came to the table, he pointed at Andy's cup. She went away, then came back with more coffee.

"Maybe I should tell you what I do," Clark said.

"Maybe. Maybe go fuck yourself."

"I'm a Maricopa County Sheriff's Deputy." Clark's hands stayed folded, his smile warm and pleasant, lifting his mustache in the corners of his mouth.

"So?"

"Your face is all over the news. Not to mention your description on all the law radios in Arizona. And not to mention," and Clark pointed towards the window, "the description of that little old ride you got parked out in the parking lot."

Andy looked down, the white plate smeared purple from the blueberry pie slices. Clark took off his hat. His dark gray hair was greased. He spread his thumb and forefinger apart across and down the sides of his mustache.

"Why'd you do it, son?"

"Do what? What the fuck are you talking about?"

"You ain't some sort of dangerous criminal, else you wouldn't have let yourself get found so easy. What made you hit the bank?" The voice was peaceful, calming, almost overwhelming. A cool canyon breeze from across the table. And Clark's eyes. They had a shine, a sparkle. Life. They loved.

"You got sick family? Debts you ain't settled? Not drugs, is it?"

"Fun, I guess." The words slipped out of Andy's mouth almost before they clicked in his brain and he realized as soon as he heard himself say them that they were right. It was like a gong going off deep in his soul. "Yeah, fun."

"Help me understand, son. Armed robbery, and it's a financial institution now so that makes things federal, but armed robbery is a kick for you?"

"Yeah." Andy looked at Clark's face, then down. He shrugged, then spread his arms out wide. "That's all I can think of. Fun. I did it for fun."

"Like a thrill."

"Yeah, like a thrill."

They were both quiet, Clark watching Andy and Andy, head in hand now, watching the coffee slosh around as he swirled his cup.

Finally, Clark said, "You know, they got things like parachute clubs. Hang gliding. Race cars."

Andy looked up. Clark was smiling. Then they both laughed, low laughter, chuckles that blended in with the talk all around them, talk which rose with the coffee steam and the cigarette smoke and the smell of frying bacon and eggs and potatoes.

"Well," Clark said.

"Well."

"I guess you know I got a job to do now."

Andy stared at his coffee cup. "Yeah."

"I'm sorry, son."

"It's okay."

Clark unfolded his hands, put them palms down on the table. He said, "I'd really think—"

He didn't finish. Couldn't. The last bullet cut through his gut, blasted out his kidney, bored through the wood of the booth, popped through the wrist of a blue-haired lady sitting the next booth over, angled up and thunked into the plaster wall. Little white shards went spinning. Under the table, Andy's hand was shaking so bad he dropped the gun. It clunked off his boot and settled in the shadows next to some torn-up Equal packets. Clark pitched forward onto the table with a grunt. His fingers moved like he was trying to grab something, grab anything. Then his arm twitched and a peppershaker went flying. The blue-haired lady was screaming in pulses of noise—up and down and up and down went her voice. Andy jumped to his feet and backed away from the table, mouth hanging open, eyes wide and round as the rim of the coffee cup. A puddle of blood was spreading between Clark's boots and the blue-haired lady had fallen onto the floor and turned onto her back, kicking like a cockroach. She scooted over the linoleum like a cockroach too and her hand was limp, dragging along behind her, gray and loose, as she wiggled along. Clark tried to stand, couldn't, then fidgeted and grunted again. His hands relaxed and quit moving altogether. The lady moved past Andy, swimming over the floor backstroke style, blood laid out like strings floating on the tiles in her wake. He took a big step back. Then another and another, until he banged into a table and fell into a fat cowboy's lap. The fat cowboy looked at him, smooth jowls trembling, and Andy jumped back to his feet. Nobody moved. Nothing but stares. A phone beeped. Somebody hiccupped. The chimes above the door tinkled.

"Oh my—" the waitress said, and the rest of her words trailed off.

ABOUT THE AUTHOR

Paul Luikart was born and raised in Ohio, and lived in Chicago for many years. He currently lives in Chattanooga, Tennessee, with his wife and children, where he directs an emergency shelter for homeless families.

A master of the realist short story, Luikart's writing has appeared in a variety of literary magazines. He also writes a twice-monthly column on social and political issues for nooga.com, an online newspaper based in Chattanooga.

Animal Heart is Luikart's first published collection of stories.

ACKNOWLEDGEMENTS

I am overwhelmed with gratitude to these people: Gregory Wolfe, Robert Clark, Gina Ochsner, and Jeanine Hathaway at Seattle Pacific University's MFA program; Gary Wilson, Patrick Somerville, Cecilia Pinto, and Stephanie Friedman at the University of Chicago's Writers' Studio; Michael McGregor at the Collegeville Institute; David Schloss, Dave Kajganich, and Eric Goodman at Miami University.

Thank you to Mom, Dad, and Sara, who have always encouraged me to tell stories.

Thank you to Pete and Kris, who allowed a writer into their family.

Thank you to the -.-. --- -... .-. .- Brothers who've seen all of these stories and without whom this book could not have been written.

Thank you to Imogen, Ingrid, and the wee one on the way.

Thank you most of all to Emily. This one's for you.

ABOUT HYPERBOREA

Hyperborea is an independent book publisher based in Canada.

Visit us online at hyperboreapub.com, and follow us on Facebook and Twitter (@HyperboreaBooks).

Read more. Read better.

CPSIA information can be obtained
at www.ICGtesting.com
Printed in the USA
LVOW07s0735020517
532927LV00002B/672/P